CORK CITY LIBRARY

Tel: (021) **4277110**
Hollyhill Library: 4392998

This book is due for return on the last date stamped below.
Overdue fines: 10c per week plus postage.

Class no. ...... *TEN* ......   Accn no. ...... 4613070 ......

SYLVIA AND TED

SYLVIA AND TED

Emma Tennant

This large print book is published by BBC Audiobooks Ltd, Bath, England and by Thorndike Press, Waterville, Maine, USA.

Published in 2003 in the U.K. by arrangement with Mainstream Publishing Company (Edinburgh) Ltd.

Published in 2003 in the U.S. by arrangement with Henry Holt and Company, LLC.

U.K. Hardcover   ISBN 0–7540–7308–4   (Chivers Large Print)
U.K. Softcover   ISBN 0–7540–7309–2   (Camden Large Print)
U.S. Softcover   ISBN 0–7862–5721–0   (General Series)

The text of this Large Print edition is unabridged.
Other aspects of the book may vary from the original edition.

Set in 16 pt. New Times Roman.

Printed in Great Britain on acid-free paper.

British Library Cataloguing in Publication Data available

Library of Congress Control Number: 2003106609

For Karl and Jane Miller
with thanks for advice and encouragement

and for Elizabeth (Compton) Sigmund

Author's Note

Sylvia and Ted is the story of the twentieth century's most famous—and most tragic—literary love affair, the marriage and separation of Sylvia Plath and Ted Hughes.

Events described in the book are based on fact, but *Sylvia and Ted* is, nevertheless, a work of the imagination. In this edition, certain revisions have been made.

The Letting Go

London, 11 February 1963

She walks up the stairs for the last time and opens the door to the flat on the second floor of the house in Fitzroy Road.

It is late—past midnight—and so dark and cold, you'd think there was nothing out there beyond the windows which throw back only the reflection of a haunting: a woman who is very pale, still young, already half transparent in light flat and white as the frozen landscape she can no longer see.

A river of scarlet runs across the floor of the room where she has elected not to sleep, the room so cold that frost climbs with arthritic fingers on windowpanes and sheets and pillows give off their smell of damp into bitter-tasting air. The red cord on the floor makes a gash— like a smiling mouth in a perfect face, like a scar high on the cheek of a woman who lies where she has fallen—and she stays a while looking down at it. The curtains she must make! The pillars of stiff material which are close to being ready to go up! But she turns, and leaves the room, also for the last time.

Really, it's quite easy, taping round the

doors after she has tiptoed into the room where the children sleep and put cups of milk down beside them. It's like the time when she was living down in the country still and took toys in socks to her babies who were too young to open or play with them when Christmas morning came. She had a family, then. Now, as she frames the doorway with the strong white tape, she is as alone as all must be, who die. She stands away from the door, stuffs towels where the old Hampstead house might let the gas in, and knows the rest of this place as her tomb. Downstairs, old Professor Thomas shuffles one more time out into the hall, then goes back inside again.

ONE

Three Childhoods and a Suicide

The Oceanic Feeling

27 April 1935

It's a beautiful sunny day. Maybe it's the first day of summer, but there are no boats yet on the water and it's just as cold and grey far out as ever it was before the beginning of this day of secrets.

Even Sylvia's favourite pebbles—those amethysts in an earlobe of white stone that sparkle and glow at low tide don't know yet that the yellow flowers are out on the broom and that the sand by the edge of the cliffs is almost warm. Once the sludge of winter down by the tidemark lightens in colour like drying hair and disintegrates into a million particles in the sun, Sylvia's stones will lose their shine, become no more than the beach detritus Grammy Schober makes you empty from sandals and pockets before entering the house. So, in their last moment of unknowing, in their bright, purple, glistening innocence, Sylvia picks up her stones and watches the sea-brightness fade from them as she holds them in her hand. Then she runs to the shore and her arms swing high over her head in the effort to throw them in as far as she can. She can tell from the litter brought up by the waves that there will be further treasure today: mussel shells, the indigo fingernails of a drowned princess, a starfish bringing a sudden pinkness from the sea.

Sylvia can tell also that something is being kept back from her at the house.

She's two and a half years old and her kind Gramper is a few yards away down the beach, sunning himself. He wears a white shirt and grey, baggy trousers and he holds a newspaper a few inches from his face. He is 'keeping an eye' on Sylvia as she picks out her stones and runs sometimes too near to that wall of water she is forbidden to enter alone. (But she never goes right in, not since the time, as a baby, she tried to crawl to that green, choking oblivion; felt the need so strong to go through to the other side, a place she knows and yet has never seen.) That time Aurelia, her mother, pulled her back. She knows Sylvia's simultaneous need for escape, adventure—and a place to hide, to be lost, to fall into a prenatal sleep.

The truth is, Sylvia knows that Gramper is hiding nothing from her. If he knows something, he's put it from his mind. He is simply there, down by the cliff where the April sun is at its strongest. He reads a local Massachusetts newspaper—but he mutters to himself in German from time to time and the low, guttural sounds come down over the wet gravel to his little granddaughter like the gulls pecking at their nests in the hard clay over his head. Gramper has no secrets—or if he has

6

they're easily discovered: his pipe stuck in the crook of a tree and a prize if Sylvia can find it; a batch of Easter eggs in bright paper in an obvious makeshift nest in a bush. There is nothing confusing or hidden about Gramper Schober.

It's the house, especially the kitchen, that has a new aura of mystery. The door of the big old-fashioned cooking range opens and trays of biscuits and loaves of bread come out burned—and Grammy Schober has never burned her bread. And when she's not absent-minded like that there's an atmosphere of excited, almost martial efficiency: tunes are hummed, the clock tick-tocks in time to the kneading and thumping and strong, firm flattening out of the belly of the dough. The big, brown Bakelite wireless, with its bulletins and weather forecasts and snippets of local news, is turned on and off as if it's telling Grammy Schober quite useless pieces of information, telling her everything except what she most wants to know. It all gives Sylvia a worried, empty feeling, as if she's about to be told of some absence, some sudden inexplicable hole.

Somehow Sylvia senses that this is the last day of her oneness with the world. She will never again live in harmony with her stones and shells and never again walk up the lawn to the house with its short, tufty grass without thinking, in an agony of self-consciousness: I'm

7

walking on a lawn. Worst, she suspects with an intolerable fear that even in the water she will be apart from it: a breathing, wriggling something else whom the ocean will not love or hold, but will spit out crashing on the stones or force under. The sea will have more fondness for its spume than for Sylvia.

So the first day of summer—an egg-yolk light playing on Gramper as he sits on the beach quite unaware of her terror—leaves Sylvia as dull and lifeless as her purple stones when they've been too long from the sea. And there is no perspective in the flat beach or the angular cliff or the sun stuck in a high round dazzle in the sky. It can all be near or millions of miles away, it can be real or just a child's drawing superimposed on the much more potent reality of the kitchen to which Sylvia must now return for lunch. The kitchen, dark and deep in Sylvia's mind, with a priestess and a hissing cauldron and a secret about to rise steaming from the pot.

*　　　*　　　*

Three weeks is a long time when you're the age Sylvia is now. A long time because you can't count yet—or, if you can, it's only in the numbing total of absences those twenty-one days and nights make up: no kisses from the mother; no stories; and no great hug from the father when he comes home. No briefcase opening to spill out a gift bought especially for her, or—and imagining this makes her swallow the tears that hurt her sinuses and bring back a whole winter of complaint and colds to her aching—eyes if there is a black briefcase, then when it is opened it is empty. There is nothing there.

A black hole opens up. Sylvia stands so straight and still, staring out to sea, that even Gramper wonders and glances up at her. But she's a good girl, really. She's looking at the buoy, very likely, as it bobs up and down in the waves that never leave it be. Or she's seen a 'whale', a whale she has pretended to see ever since the big whale was beached here last year.

Sylvia has tried to draw the dark, blobby whale that swims along the farthest boundary of her watery world. The whale is her mother, carrying a dark secret over dangerous deep water where Sylvia is not allowed to go.

And when the humped, fat mass of the black-bodied whale has gone over the horizon, Sylvia cries inconsolably until it's time to go home.

Of course, Grammy Schober has noticed that Sylvia is becoming increasingly upset by this separation from her parents. The child's attention wanders now when she's read a story. And the arrangements she makes from odds and ends Grammy finds her in cupboards and jars—string, buttons, paper clips, little fragments of wool from a long-outworn pullover—are straight and symmetrical, showing none of the flowery inventiveness of her earlier 'patterns'. It's time the child went home.

And now—today—as of this very minute, when Sylvia walks sullen up from the beach and Gramper walks beside her, tries in vain to amuse her with the shapes he makes from the newspaper: scarecrow, bunny rabbit with floppy ears, house of print with four empty squares for windows—here, now, the poor child can be told she'll be home again soon.

How they'll hug! How they'll kiss!

Grammy Schober flies around the kitchen, and her new energy, the energy of life, of birth, of a world starting all over again, brings the sun dancing in in stripes so that Sylvia, quietly appearing in the doorway, sees a tiger running in the well-ordered kitchen with its cabinets and mugs and pots and pans all gleaming, as Grammy insists on having them.

Sylvia watches the tiger as Grammy tells her 'the wonderful news'. She sees a tray of gingerbread men lifted from the big black oven and laid on the table: is this 'the special treat' Grammy has been promising her? Sylvia is worried, and her eyes look up at Grammy. There's a stew in the pot atop the stove. Is that her lunch? She wants her lunch, this is the wrong time for a gingerbread man. In her mind she sees herself throwing up the stew, a pile of shaming, smelling vomit right there on

10

the kitchen table, with a half-eaten carrot sticking out of the top. Guilty already—for she knows now she will vomit, in this new atmosphere that holds its secret like the whale on the line of sea as it meets the grey sky— homesick and guilty, Sylvia begins to bawl.

As grown-ups will so often react when children are overexcited, her screams bring laughter and protestations—'You'll be all right . . . Darling Sivvy, haven't you understood, darling? There, there . . .'—and handkerchiefs of Austrian linen, huge and white, are mopping her tears, coming down on her head: peek-a-boo!

But all to no avail. Sylvia's tears dry, but the new energy in the house fills her with a destructive, tearing pace: a race from the warm, stifling kitchen of baking tins and tiny biscuit men with their foolish outstretched arms and legs—a run so fast that Gramper and Grammy Schober will never catch her—to the sea.

And as she runs, knowing already that she is dead to the world—knowing that her purple, white-rimmed stones, even if wet and gleaming from the rising tide, will still be just stones, their living jewel—brightness, their speech, their cries of pain, all taken away from her now—as she runs she hears Grammy's voice again and again, like a radio stuck on with terrible news.

A baby! A baby brother!

On the far side of the sea, where the hills stop and the great forest of water lies flat—where the sea becomes the sky—a whale moves slowly, a double black hump. Then it dives down and the flat unwavering line of the horizon runs across Sylvia's gaze like a scalpel going in. Sylvia turns and walks gravely along the line of hard wet sand where the tide advances in semicircles like eyebrows raised higher and higher in surprise.

*   *   *

Arms hold another—a bundle—and Sylvia sees a black emptiness, a rival: it can have no features, it is the other, it is the unnecessary, inescapable thing.

Her father's hands, and the bumblebees that love to feel safe in the warm, male prison of her father's hands, buzzing contentedly for Sylvia and her father alone—Look! They won't sting this kindly giant of a man!—her father's hands hold and embrace the rival and Sylvia is forever cast out of Eden. Her mother, unforgivable perpetrator of this great betrayal, is blotted from sight as she walks along the landing, comes down the stairs to say that the bath is run and waiting, wafts her faint scent that is like lime trees across the hall as she goes out to fetch Sylvia in the garden.

Sylvia isn't there. She wills their cries of fear at her disappearance.

And sure enough, the cries are real: Grammy and Gramper hurrying along the beach as fast as their years will permit them.

Sylvia feels no pity for them. She bends down, picks up a starfish washed in by this new tide. She holds the small red hand in her palm.

She is quiet and thoughtful when the Schobers catch up with her at last. Standing still, quite composed. And as they come to lead her gently to the car for her journey home, Grammy notes with a certain relief that Sylvia is not insisting today on carting her collection of stones and mussel shells and what have you on her journey back to her parents.

You can't be too careful with a new baby Grammy thinks, as Sylvia drops the starfish on the beach and doesn't look back once at the dead hand of her murdered newborn brother.

Berlin, 1935

Across the ocean the little girl has never even seen, in a country to which her mother belongs and her father decidedly does not, the little girl is listening to a story before being put to bed. She knows it well—it is 'Little Red Riding Hood', the story her mother, from the heartland of German Protestantism, loves best. But the little girl has noticed that her father gets anxious and upset when he hears it read aloud in the strong, pure voice his wife has when she delves into the tales of her own childhood. The little girl's father is Russian: the forest Red Riding Hood enters is alien to him. Worse, though the little girl has only the faintest inkling of the reason why the kind Dr Gutman clears his throat and paces in the over-ornamented parlour below as his wife's voice floats down to him, there is always the sound of a door opening and then closing when Lisa gets to the end, the wolf dressed up as dear old Granny. The little girl, who is the apple of Dr Gutman's eye, hates it when he opens the door and closes it behind him. It means he's gone out for at least an hour, to try to wear off the anxiety the story appears to induce in him. The little girl, who is seven years old, is Assia Gutman. She's torn between wanting the story again, and keeping her adored father in the house for the rest of the evening.

Tonight, despite the usual build-up of almost unbearable suspense as Red Riding Hood ends her walk through the wood and goes up the path to the door of her grandmother's cottage, there is no sound of Dr Gutman pacing in the study downstairs. As Lisa reads, her brow furrows: it's almost as if the walking to and fro, followed by the front door opening and closing, have become a part of the story, and the excitement of 'What big teeth you have, Granny!' won't be the same without them. 'What big eyes you have—' Lisa dutifully begins, but her voice is losing its confident ring. Even her little daughter looks perplexed, and keeps glancing at the bedroom door as if she thinks her father might be hiding behind there, transformed suddenly into a wicked wolf, when she has loved and trusted him all her life.

Dr Gutman is an orthopaedic surgeon, and people with bad backs and twisted limbs come frequently to his consulting room, on the ground floor next to the study. That's what has happened (both Lisa Gutman and Assia think this in unison): while the story was being read, they didn't hear the doorbell and an emergency patient coming in. That's where Lonya must be—down behind the thick mahogany door, pulling and pushing at legs or arms, manipulating a back so that its owner can, quite unexpectedly, find himself sitting upright and straight on the long, thin table.

Assia is displeased when her father's attention is turned away from her. She likes to feel he's as frightened of what nearly happens to Red Riding Hood as she is. She just wishes he'd wait for the happy ending, when the wolf's stomach is slit open and Granny steps out, smiling, instead of going out of the house; or, in this case, permitting a patient to take precedence over the demands of his darling daughter.

Lisa finishes the story, though both teller and listener are restless and uneasy. Here comes the big knife!—Assia screams with

15

pretend fear as the wolf jumps snarling from its disguise in Granny's bed. But even the lacy frills at the wolf's hairy wrists don't absorb the pretty little girl as much as they usually do. She doesn't even wait for the last, triumphant thrust at the cornered animal, and slides from her child's bed to the floor. Somehow she must find her Tatti: she's burst in on a few occasions when he's been busy in his consulting room, but he never really minds.

'Lonya!' Now Mutti is calling her husband when he's in consultation, something she has never been known to do. 'Lonya, send the child straight up to bed, I ask you!'

By now the little girl has reached the foot of the stairs and is running in the sweet little harlequin slippers Mutti gave her for her birthday, back when it was sunny May. Now it's dark and as frightening in the hall as it is in the forest when Red Riding Hood first meets the wolf. Where is Tatti? He doesn't keep the hall dark, does he?—unless of course he went out hours ago, when it was still light. The complication of the thought halts the child a moment, by the open door of the empty consulting room.

There's no one in the study, either. Assia runs to the front door and stands staring at it a moment or two before laying a podgy hand on the big gilt doorknob. There's one place— she's been taken there by her father lots of times—where he's likely to be found. At old

16

Uncle Victor's—he's a doctor, too, and specialises in children. It's not far to go. And she wouldn't sleep anyway, unless the one person she wants in the world is there to ruffle her hair and whisper good night and turn off the lights before going quietly down the stairs.

The street is cold and white, with its dusting of ice and snow. The child runs, so fast she doesn't feel the cold in her nightdress and checkered dressing-gown. The street already begins to look unfamiliar, and the chimney pots on the old, crooked houses stick up like trees in a forest. All the lights in the windows are out—but a child her age wouldn't wonder why. The path hasn't been trodden for some time: there are no footprints in this deserted, freezing wood.

The fire can't be seen until she rounds the corner; it's hidden by a tall building just as empty and abandoned-looking as the rest. The fire sends tongues of bright flame up into the starless sky. And there, like stone men marching without eyes, ears, or hearts, are soldiers holding torches. The procession, loud and muffled at the same time, like the drums the little girl used to enjoy hearing in parades when her mother and father still took her to the town square, comes toward her like a long column of fear.

Why can't she wake up? That can't be Uncle Victor, stumbling behind the procession, in shabby trousers and no jacket in this midwinter night? And—surely—that can't be—

'Lonya!' The mother's voice is near now, four pairs of hands seize the child and she's whisked down the street to the safety of her own front door and the longed-for smell of plum pudding and mince pie.

Why are they taking Uncle Victor away? How did her father, sole witness of his friend's abduction—unable to prevent it, powerless at the force of the Nazis as they continue their crusade of Judenrein, cleansing the Fatherland of Jews—succeed in escaping, and rescuing his wife and daughter too?

This is a story that's never told. The lamps in the hall are lit when the Gutman family returns home. The evening has to go on, and it does.

But the child doesn't forget the forest she ran into that night. The stone men think they're rescuing Germany from the wolf—and Assia has learned that her father, like Uncle Victor, is seen as the evil creature that will eat little children alive. For the first time in her young life Assia lies awake all night. She's more frightened, in her own safe little room, than she ever can be again when the story of 'Little Red Riding Hood' is read aloud.

Killing is an Art

He climbs meticulously over the fine rain of gravel that comes down in an avalanche by the side of the ravine. He looks down, triumphant as the fall increases; giddy; heart stopping suddenly when a peregrine falcon hangs above him in the blue Yorkshire sky.

The boy has a knowledge of these hills and moors. He is as much a part of them as the life only he can see, hidden in ling and bracken or deep in the dark hole that appears as a gash on the mountain's flank, earth kept fresh by nocturnal tunnelling, as bare as a mining scar by day.

He feels the pulse of hare and rabbit, fox and deer. He is a hunter. He stands still in that suspended second when he kills, when life stops along with his own breath. Then come the warm feathers of wood pigeon, crow, or grouse; spilled blood, eyes still bright, inquiring even after death.

He hires himself out sometimes as a beater, this boy whose name is Ted. He has passed the seven years of his life here under hills and crags, along the side of brown rushing rivers that carry ice-cold foam down from the highest treeless peaks. He will leave here soon, and will no longer be a part of this world that is Mytholmroyd. But seven years is long enough

19

to learn the track of every beast and bird. And to learn, too, a way of hiding from the lords of all this creation: landowners, gamekeepers, those who rear and trap and kill.

Beaters fan out across the moor. Ted rubs his hands, numb with rain and cold from a long day raising fodder for the guns. Cluck . . . cluck . . . shuish—he knows the sounds that will get grouse or pheasant rising slowly, gracelessly, to meet their death. His hands no longer feel the rough staff he cut from ash, halfway down the valley. He walks up the cliffside, and tiny pebbles, falling at the probing of the stick, go down like squibs in a burst of rattling shot.

He doesn't know how he did it, the boy who comes up to fish the rivers in the high regions, where wild nasturtiums glint red and gold in summer, and in winter icicles linger like children's fishing rods left standing by the side of the beck. He doesn't know why he forgot he was out beating that day, on land where everything belongs to the one man and neither bird, animal, nor tree can possess its own soul. It was the cold, perhaps, and hail that, even in the season of days so long the boy's eyes fade before the light goes, swept across the moors, bouncing off puddles and bogland, making a veil of hard, white lace in front of his eyes.

Whatever the reason, the boy killed a deer. The men are in his father's front room now, asking questions. Did this young lad know what he had done? Does he realise he put himself in danger, along with damaging the property of the owner of the estate? Can the boy explain himself, please? Will he come with them, down to the station, and answer questions, please?

The deer had come just at the edge of the larch trees, and stood a few seconds as the white rain fanned out around it on the moor behind a windbreak of pine and spruce. The antlers were what the boy saw first. Was it a roebuck? How long he has yearned, with his great lust to kill, to take one of these, lift it dead like a bride in his arms and carry it down the mountainside. He knows that the deer knows this, as it stands there, momentarily unsure.

How can a beater have a rifle concealed about his person? Who was responsible for giving a boy that age a gun? A .22, loaded, ready to shoot: an old gun but a rifle all the same.

The boy's father doesn't know. Ted goes out on the hills and moors all day—during the school holidays, of course. And in all weathers. He just doesn't know.

The deer fell when the boy fired, and then it ran, or tried a scamper, a grotesque parody of agony, then ran again, outlined against dull brown heather and now in a clear light, the blizzard weaving its way south down the valley.

And now the deer fell once more and rolled over and died and the boy stood on the overgrown path only he had been able to decipher, in the moss and bracken, and found he was unable to go up to the deer.

I just don't understand, the landowner says. He sits in a high-backed chair near a blazing log fire. All around him are trophies of his killing days: stuffed ptarmigan, dead salmon coffined in glass; stags' antlers high up on the walls. He must have had the gun stowed away somewhere, the landowner says. Confiscate it. They're leaving soon, aren't they, for Mexborough? Then just leave it at that.

The boy's father sleeps badly that night. It's not the first time: the big ship sails on toward the low shore, in his dream, and he can see the enemy in the scrub, on sand dunes above blue water. He's been waiting months with the rest for this moment, when the cutters are sent to the shore, at Gallipoli.

Ted hears his father cry out in his sleep. One of only a handful of survivors of the ill-fated 1915 campaign, this man who is still in his early middle age could be old, a veteran of all the wars of history.

The cutters came back with the dead soldiers. You cleaned the blood out of the cutters and you carried on.

The boy's father cries out, then the dream passes again.

In all the boy's childhood there is killing. The love of killing, the acceptance and necessity of killing. How can he tell what he must kill and what should be left alive? Why shouldn't he imitate the power of the man who owns the land and on it each living thing?

In Ted's dream later that night, the deer comes back to life.

In the terrible darkness of the wood at night he sees its soft eyes pleading. He leans down to pick it up: his heart leaps with joy. The deer is only wounded; he'll take it home.

But as he lifts it, he sees that he holds a lovely young woman in his arms, not a deer. And as he gazes down into her face, she dies.

Persephone

Wellesley, Massachusetts, 2 June 1953

Sylvia must not fail. Her mother, Aurelia, knows it. Her brother, Warren, knows it. Her teachers (so Sylvia thinks, at least) all know it, only too well. Even the queen of England, whose coronation is to be shown on TV today, knows the price exacted for failure. Sixty years in a mental institution! You couldn't see that happening to a queen.

Aurelia is with friends on this baking hot day. She's not outside, on the bristly green lawn of 34 Elwood Street, where Grammy Schober lies, deciding to stay home and have Warren bring her lemonade when she desires it. No, Aurelia is indoors, at her friends' house, watching the little monochrome figure of the queen as she makes her way up the aisle, the very picture of sanity and poise. If only poor Sivvy were more like the queen! How pretty the lady-in-waiting is, who—as Aurelia fantasises—has hair the colour of corn! What a shame Sivvy is so wrapped up in herself she couldn't come!

But Sylvia has failed. Without prizes, without admission to the world of literature (and she has failed in this, too: momentously, this summer, she was refused admission to Harvard), she must spare her mother the shame of her relentless inability to succeed. She must go, not leave a trace of the burden, the embarrassment, she has become.

Where will she go? To Germany, to the Polish Corridor, to the family of her dead and longed-for father, Otto, where Sylvia, speechless in the tongue she fears and loves, will be regarded as a failure? Not possible. To England, where the poetry she longs to write awaits her? No, that won't do: another brainless student washed up on the White Cliffs, incapable of writing so much as her own name? Who'll want her, when she has neither rhyme nor reason? Who'll pay for a long lifetime in the snake pit, when Otto's death has left Aurelia and her loving son impoverished?

The sun is so blazing hot today that it fries

24

Sylvia's hand as she stands on tiptoe on the stool in Aurelia's bedroom and reaches out to open the wardrobe's topmost door. It comes through a chink in the blind so carefully lowered by her mother before she went out to see the queen. It lights up the flat, complacent wedge of cream-painted wood that is the top section of the wardrobe, with the two little white china handles that say: open me if you dare. Although Sylvia is nearly twenty-one years old, she has never dared. Aurelia's strongbox is in there—and when she was a child the word 'strongbox' meant for little Sivvy the witch Baba-Yaga in the forest, the witch who has iron teeth. Try to steal your mother's strongbox and you'll get eaten alive.

Today, perhaps because of the sizzling sun that beams in through the chink where the blind is uneven (the blind is a failure, too: why hasn't the defect been noticed and repaired?), Sylvia's thoughts are far from punishment or retribution. Her hand shows up pink and translucent in the dreadful heat of the sun. She thinks of the death by electrocution this summer of the Rosenbergs—atomic spies, so they said—and she feels her nerves shriek, the seconds turn to minutes as the great rays seize her brain and heart. If Sylvia weren't always going to fail, she'd have fought for the Rosenbergs.

What would they do with someone who, so spectacularly, fails? (For, as ever, Sylvia must refer the pain and horror back to herself.) Will they arrest her, lock her up for eternity, as the only way of dealing with one so useless to society? While there's time—maybe only today, the here and now, remains to her—she'll commit her very last act of independence. As the queen crawls back down the aisle of the abbey, laden with the insignia of her wealth and majesty, Sylvia will start to die.

*   *   *

It's a shock, at first, to find that her mother's strongbox is flimsy and small, and could be broken open by a child. But then, Sylvia feels—and never more keenly than today— that she is just that: a feeble and dependent child. Aurelia did nothing to deserve this monstrosity of a grown woman unable to sustain herself in an adult world.

As in a fairy tale, the little key is quickly found, in the jewellery drawer Sylvia would stand gazing at while her mother fastened ear clips, laid a necklace of semiprecious stones around her neck, before going out to dine with her husband.The child of parents in love with each other is an orphan: the words of Robert Louis Stevenson, swallowed in the great bouts of reading Sylvia has undertaken since she was old enough to learn words and their magic meanings, come to haunt her as she fits the key into the lock. The box opens; the bottle of pills lies inside. Brand new! Fifty coloured capsules of death.

*   *   *

Up in the world of the living, the letter is propped against a bowl on the table in the hall. Sylvia is going for a long walk. Not to be waited for. Perhaps not back until the next day. That is all it says. And Aurelia stands gazing at it, sick with the knowledge that her premonition was correct. That as the coronation of the Queen of England flickered on in the little black-and-white TV her own daughter would fly from her; disappear; go underground. But, unfortunately, Aurelia doesn't hear this clue from her unconscious mind and instead, with shaking hand, lifts the heavy Bakelite receiver and phones the police. Comb the streets! Here are contact numbers in New York! But as she speaks, she feels the emptiness of the search.

*   *   *

In the underworld, it is dark and barricaded with the logs Sylvia pulled aside in this cavern under the porch and then rearranged to bar the gate to hell. The underworld fills with the sound of the dead, as they chirrup and whisper in the damp, dusty air.

She eats the pills, fast at first and then

27

slowly. She sees the river as it coils away from her, and the dim outlines of boats carrying the newly dead, their faces white and appalled.

She hears the squeak of bats, souls roosting in the cinderblock underporch Otto had built on the house, an addition he knew would give shade in summer, in the hot, sultry weather his Teutonic nature doesn't suit. He couldn't have known that the log store beneath would hold his daughter, form a tomb in which her desperate mother would never think of seeking her.

Sylvia sleeps; but on the third day, as her mother and brother sit above her in their collapsed world—as they raise food and water to lips too parched to speak, as they turn to stone in the cooling lava of Sylvia's wicked and thoughtless disappearance from the normal, the ordered, the everyday—they hear a moan from ten feet below.

'Sylvia,' Aurelia says. In their minds, the mother and brother compress the vast distances of America, the rapes and kidnaps and mountains where snow lingers all year round. 'Sylvia,' Aurelia says. And they run down to the homely log store under the porch.

And later, when the River Styx flows in the hospital where Sylvia lies—only a scar on her cheek, where she had lain on the floor, visible evidence of her failure, her latest fall from grace—she knows it as dangerous and live. It is an electric current that will jolt her, so they say, back to sanity. But all the patient thinks of as she lies in the white room is this: that this is the summer of another failed attempt, this time at death; and that this is the summer they electrocuted Julius and Ethel Rosenberg.

Tel Aviv, 1944

It's Christmas, and the decorations are going up in the Gutman household. As it's a preponderantly Jewish neighbourhood, eyebrows rise too: but Dr Gutman is respected for running a smart, up-to-date clinic, and no one really minds. Lisa, Dr Gutman's wife, is homesick for Germany, for the songs and hymns Jews everywhere have learned to dread. Out of tact, perhaps, Lisa doesn't go for a carol service on Christmas Eve. Instead, strains of 'La Vie en Rose' and the latest foxtrots and quicksteps blare from the villa where the family has been comfortably ensconced since fleeing Berlin eight years ago. The reason for the loudness of the music (it's obvious that someone keeps turning down the volume on the expensive walnut radio-gramophone and that someone else keeps turning it up again) can be seen through the windows of the pretty old Colonial house. A girl who waltzes and quicksteps with a besotted young British airman is the cause of the inconsiderate and ear-splitting sound emanating from Dr Gutman's. She is Assia, now sixteen years old and a beauty who is compared to Hedy Lamarr (by the young airforce sergeant) and Cleopatra (by her besotted father).

Whatever Assia wants, Assia gets. She pays scant attention to the complaints of her sister, Celia, older and lacking Assia's devastating looks, when Celia complains that she can't get on with the game of chess she plays every day in the dining-room with her best friend, Hannah Zlotopolsky, if the dance music is kept at this unbearable level. Assia turns and twirls in the flared silk skirt Lisa made for her demanding daughter, kneeling on the floor and cutting out the shiny fabric with a huge pair of scissors brought all the way from Germany. As Assia twists her agile young body, and the music changes tempo to a jitterbug, the skirt takes on a life of its own and sails up between the thighs of the handsome young mechanic like a ship in full sail; the electricity causes him for a second to let go of Assia's hand, and she jitterbugs right off into a corner of the parquet-floored room. A snigger comes from the doorway, pushed open a couple of inches, as Celia and Hannah look in. But what does Assia care? With beauty such as hers, other girls can laugh if they want to.

The airforce sergeant's name is John Steel. He has brilliantined hair and thick lips, which make him look like a crooner. He has a vague idea that Assia is using him for her own purposes, but he's too dim to work out what these are. She frequently hints that she'd love more than anything in the world to go to London—where he, John Steel, is from and where he will return when his service in Palestine is done. Can she be hinting, too, that she'd like to marry him? He'd do anything for Assia, just anything. And now that she's sixteen, she can marry him—not, actually, that he's got as far yet as working this out.

While the dancing goes on, Dr Gutman comes out of his study and shoos the giggling and envious elder sister and the bespectacled Hannah away from their spying place by the door to what will be tonight's ballroom. Muttering, Hannah pulls a slab of halvah from her pocket and breaks off a powdery couple of inches for Celia. Dr Gutman frowns. Recompensed for the lack of an exciting life they can already clearly see in the future, the girls mooch out into the calm garden, where lemon and orange trees give the air of a paradise, a place where nothing bad can ever happen. Dr Gutman watches the girls go into a grove and sit disconsolately on a bench. Now, as he turns back to face the open French windows of the ballroom, he sees Assia, not knowing she is observed, as she swoops out on the arm of John Steel. She pauses dramatically on the top step: it's obvious she's doing her Scarlett O'Hara number, Vivien Leigh and Ashley just before the big ball at Twelve Oaks.

The girls on their bench in the grove look up, make faces of disgust, and look down again at their stubby fingers. Dr Gutman makes to walk forward—he's hidden by a corner of the handsome stone house he has been fortunate enough to acquire—then stops in his tracks. His daughter, the apple of his eye, Assia, is kissing the young airforce sergeant—and, as Dr Gutman notes with anguish, she's kissing as if she has done it plenty of times before.

The main reason, apart from fatherly affection, for Lonya Gutman's distress is his fear that Assia will discontinue her education entirely. He knows her to be an exceptionally clever girl: she's been writing poetry since she was eight years old and has no difficulty understanding geometry or science at the school she attends, where British officers send their children. Surely Assia can be persuaded to stay on another two years—then, he promises her, he'll help her get to Oxford or Cambridge: how about that? But Assia looks mutinous when the subject of her further education comes up. And when she looks mutinous, she's even prettier than Vivien Leigh. Poor Dr Gutman, he fears for his daughter: she has such violent alterations of mood. Lisa says they're to be expected at her age, but Dr Gutman knows they go beyond what is considered normal adolescent changeability. When Assia gets too excited, he has to give her an injection to calm her down.

What's happening now on the steps leading from the French windows into the garden looks to Lonya like a signal that an injection may be needed later. Assia is laughing, and flirting (he can't think of any other word for it), and her eyes, dark and shining, are fixed on the youthful mechanic like (again Dr Gutman is at a loss for words) those of an owl about to capture a small night rodent. Leading him by the hand, Asssa now descends the stone stairs, and the lovers (Dr Gutman earnestly prays they are not) make their way to the conservatory. Lonya told Lisa two years ago she should not have insisted on a conservatory! Now look what is happening! In full sight of the inert and sulky Celia and Hannah, John Steel has gone down on one knee in the hot, swampy air of Dr Gutman's most costly addition to his property. The leaf of a banyan tree brushes against his cheek and partly obscures his handsome, if too wide-lipped, face. Assia is sitting on the wrought-iron bench Lisa painted in the summer, preparing the place for the Christmas Ball well in advance, as she always likes to do. Assia's hand, her delicate fingers tipped with Helena Rubinstein ruby nail polish, dangles delicately. The aspiring mechanic seizes it and presses four fingers to his oversized mouth.

Dr Gutman groans. The girls lean forward. A band of British soldiers, friends who have volunteered to come early to assist with the floodlighting Dr Gutman wants in his garden and ballroom, come through the gate at the far end of the lemon and orange grove.

Lisa Gutman, who has stepped out unseen from the French windows, waves to the fresh-faced young men in their uniforms and Sam Browne belts. I tell you, she has said to her friends, when Assia is older, one of these British officers will make a good husband for her. Lonya knows she thinks this, and he knows his remarks on education are only half heard.

Assia and John Steel emerge from the conservatory engaged to be married. The worst blow is yet to come. Tomorrow—after the party—Assia will apply for a passport to go and live with her new husband in London. Dr Gutman, in one terrible moment, sees the ruination of his daughter. And who will be in London to give her an injection?

TWO

Love and marriage

The Meeting

It's cold in Cambridge. Cambridge—cold, with the sky bright and fierce (when it's not snowing, that is, dull and white as the blankets she piles on the bed to try to keep warm). It's a masculine city, hard and beautiful and laid out in squares and rectangles that will allow no undergrowth, no prowl or sudden loss of sensation. Cambridge admonishes, stands needle-straight in fens that let in a blast of cold air from Denmark. It is a perfect place to study —as Sylvia does—the meaning of Tragedy.

Tonight is one of those nights when everything seems clogged up. A freezing mist has wandered the narrow streets all day, and what is left of it obscures the pinnacles and spires. Lights in the women's house at Whitstead—where Sylvia prepares to go out for the evening, picks through her outfits, and sighs—are dimmed by the pervading fog. From the street the place looks unwelcoming and mean. Women live here, the thin light from the windows seems to say: there is no life, no abundance. And as if to prove the point, a threadbare curtain is drawn across a window and a light just under Sylvia's room goes out. From here, say the walls of the gabled house and the patch of shrubbery where flowers refuse to grow, no woman has found happiness.

Sylvia is clogged up too. The sinus infection that returns with those thoughts of disappearance and death has made it painful to breathe, to think, to move. The motionless, bitter air has crept into her face, into her very being—and even if you stuff newspaper into the window jambs and under the doors it comes to find you, to lie beside you on the bed, which has the damp coldness of a lake. There is no escaping, even by the gas fire, even with the Cambridge dream of toasting crumpets and writing poetry to make you shiver, and falling in love as you punt on the Cam with a handsome, clever undergraduate. There is no dream, only the reality of this all-pervading cold.

*   *   *

Sylvia searches through her wardrobe for something red to wear. Red, the colour of life, of blood, of the sexual chase. Red lips in a full wide smile, redder than in the slicks, redder than the lips of a movie star. Red that pulls in a husband before it fades to the pretty pink of a nursery—but also red that can bring mayhem if you don't look out, with your life in ruins and your heart broken in two. (But she dons red all the same: it is the only answer to the

38

cold, repelling algebra of Cambridge.)

Sylvia selects an outfit that is 'all-American', neat and tailored, and her very red mouth smiles back at her in the mirror as she affixes a red hair band and adds silver earrings. Ha! No woman don now, condemned forever to a life of comment: the essays on Dorothea Casaubon to be marked neatly; the annotations to *As You Like It* to be ready by the end of the week for the Amateur Dramatic Club. No baggy cardigan, no quiet despair. This red-lipped woman, blonde hair garlanded with red, is going out to kill—and maybe, just maybe, if she strikes it lucky on this freezing February night, she will find herself in turn pursued by somebody as intent as she is on the kill.

*   *   *

In the icy air of the fens, new poems grow and prosper. They're printed with the same urgency with which they're written: and a few days ago Sylvia found a new 'little magazine', *Saint Botolph's Review*, for sale down by the bridge with a batch of exciting new poets within its covers.

Sylvia has memorised lines from the poems in the new 'review' (it looks more like a leaflet, really) and especially the work of one Ted Hughes.

And tonight there is a party—at the Women's Union in Falcon Yard—to mark the

39

first issue of the magazine. Sylvia will go. She hasn't really been invited, but she'll go all the same. To meet the man whom she knows already from the poems in *Saint Botolph's Review* to be the only man who can match Otto, the Prince, the lost father of her dreams. She has no idea what he looks like—but she knows somehow that she will know him as soon as she sees his face. Thus does Sylvia— and doesn't she relish it fully, all the schmaltz and women's magazineness of it, all the operatic inevitability of it?—go forth to meet her doom.

First, of course, she must wrap up warm. It's a mile on a bike from Whitstead to King's Parade to the centre of Cambridge and there's a fine, too, if you don't wear your gown: six shillings and eightpence to be precise, the equivalent, in 1950s terms, of a medieval groat. Under the gown she'll need at least two sweaters and long, thick socks (tights don't exist yet). To top it all, a balaclava on the head obscures the sexy red mouth, leaving visible only a nose red, this time unintentionally, from the cold. A *femme fatale* indeed. But certainly, a woman of determination.

Miller's Bar

It's dark and noisy and crowded, and Sylvia, preparing herself for the party, is tanking up with an acquaintance who recognised her under all that gear—his name is Hamish Stewart. Two whiskies, three whiskies, four— he can't help looking at her admiringly as the juices begin to flow and the colour fills her cheeks and her bright brown eyes conquer the cold of Cambridge. He wonders if she'll be too drunk to go to the party, and he decides he'll stick with her and go anyway, because he'll screw her later. And he orders her a fifth whisky and she laughs and clings to his arm and the red lips come right up close to him so that they fill his vision and he sees a scarlet galleon, a sailing ship in full sail. He tries to kiss her, but someone behind them shoves and nudges on the way to the bar . . .

'Aren't I a whore? Aren't I a slut?' Sylvia says, highly delighted with herself.

And her escort, the man who will shortly deliver her to her fate, wonders if this is the only way Sylvia can unwind: to find abandonment in a sense of her own squalor and worthlessness. This Fulbright scholar, too! He smiles and tells Sylvia she's a silly girl (and he'll say it again later; he just doesn't seem capable of picking up on her need for pain and humiliation). But for the moment—

'Let's go to the party,' Sylvia says, and she slurs her words so that Hamish has to wonder if she will really carry out her threat to shout out all these new poems she has learned by heart.

Falcon Yard

It's amazing what a good blast of icy air can do. By the time Sylvia arrives at the yard, with its tall, narrow houses on three sides, she is sober and showing a heightened beauty that seems almost unearthly—as if she has prepared herself all her life for this evening, and will make sure it is embalmed along with her, a jewel-bright memory that will become as famous as she.

She pauses by the door to the stairs up to the first-floor room. She turns toward Hamish as if she needs, instinctively, his recognition of the importance of the occasion—and then turns again and starts to go up the uncarpeted wooden stairs. Hamish follows her, thinking he has lost her already.

The room used for the Women's Union—which came into existence as a reply to the male arrogance of the Men's Union (but funds were never ample enough to provide the same comfort)—is about twenty-six feet long; tonight there's a squeezed feeling on its bare boards because it's hard to cram a combo and an uncountably large number of people into the first floor of a Victorian house. Once you've walked up those wooden stairs—the whole place stinks of fish, the Women's Union is situated above a fishmonger's shop (which serves somehow to underline the inferior status of women in this most male of cities,

42

where in the 1950s men outnumber women ten to one and sex is a rare commodity)—once up past the fishy stink and up those breakneck stairs, though, it turns out the party isn't half bad after all. Jazz, Humphrey Lyttelton style. Black polo necks for the girls, mascara-rimmed eyes, birds' nests of hair—men in black too, talking of Burroughs and Kerouac.

*   *   *

And there, at the far end of the room—Sylvia sees him while she dances wildly with Luke Myers, the heat and excitement have made her drunk again and she shouts the words of Luke's poems, for she has memorised these as well from the pages of the magazine—there stands the man she has waited all week long to see.

*   *   *

At the far end of the room is a small kitchen, with windows in the wooden walls that look onto the main room.

In the kitchen is a large scrubbed table, with bowls of punch so strong you need the icy corridors of air that make up the invisible architecture of Cambridge to carry you home late at night (there's brandy in it and wine and vodka and fruit thrown in without thought); but there's just one bottle of cognac on the table—strong, bright, and brown as Sylvia's eyes as she turns from dancing with Luke to see the stranger. The man she has come to meet crosses the floor and meets Sylvia at last and takes her outstretched hand and leads her into the kitchen and up to the bottle of cognac on the table there.

There's a rumpus going on in the little kitchen at the end of the room where the Women's Union holds its polite debates ('Does God exist?' has recently been earnestly discussed). And in 1950s Cambridge an 'incident'—as some of the more thoughtful and least sought-after female undergraduates describe it—is both unwanted and unusual. (After all, there could be trouble with the authorities.)

Luke Myers is the first to see what's going on in the kitchen, empty for the moment of all but two people, a man and a woman—but the whole scene, thanks to the windows into the main room, is clearly visible to anyone who looks in. What can be seen is so wild, so primitive, so extraordinary, that even the music dies down and people break out in excited chatter and the place grows hot—so hot that the fish smell from downstairs comes up through the floorboards and overpowers the stink of wine and punch. There's a sense of orgy—of Dionysus let loose—and of the flames that must consume such unlicensed behaviour in puritan, post-war Cambridge: the flames of hell.

There's an element of farce about it, too. After shouting the first line of his poem—'I did it, I'—Sylvia is stamping and shouting and the words pour from that red mouth and then—the fight is on—around and around the table they race, while the other partygoers, some embarrassed, some cheering them to a greater frenzy, crowd toward the kitchen and this wild display of sexual desire.

It's like a film, it's as if the parts have been written long ago and the actors have rehearsed for so long that they have become the characters they're impersonating.

Take 1. Sylvia's hair band—that ribbon of red that carries her through depression and the cold Cambridge winter, that symbol of life and lust and need—is ripped from her blonde hair.

Take 2. Her silver earrings are yanked off. Pain. She cries out. The earrings are taken as a trophy. The Christmas tree that was Sylvia is bare, denuded . . . waiting to be felled.

But—and here the camera comes in close, a hundred pairs of eyes stare in disbelief—this red-lipped woman has still her mouth as a weapon in the struggle to the death. And she approaches her adversary as a vampire— through the scarlet lips, the sharp teeth reach his cheek and bite—and as the blood trickles down they pull apart, dazed by the intensity of the fight, the absolute non-existence of anyone

45

else on this island, this pool of spotlight they have so quickly made for themselves. They turn sheepish and make their way back into the crowd.

Sylvia has drawn blood.

*   *   *

And later, as she and Hamish climb into his college and lie on the floor and make love, she can see herself as the scarlet woman at last: the biter, the tramp, the whore. She wants only to be assured that she is indeed all these things: that with her red hair she can eat men like air.

But Hamish is the practical, phlegmatic type. He tells Sylvia she's a silly girl again.

And she doesn't forgive him easily for that, not she.

Holocaust Night

13 April 1956

Friday the thirteenth. Sylvia's father's birthday. But it's his death she finds at 18 Rugby Street, on the treeless street in the low reaches of Bloomsbury where she will meet Ted today, for the first time since the party. And it's Otto's death she must commemorate now,

46

with an act of rape.

Who's raping whom, is what the lone woman wonders on the floor above. Who cries and crashes as they give their souls and lives in a meeting that was never more than a stopgap for Sylvia, on her way to Paris to find a love who has no wish to be found? Who killed Cock Robin, this time?

The house is as dirty as a past of war, and sex seized between broken appointments, and glasses hazed with unwashed breaths, can make it. It's like a house on a seaside pier: put in a penny and see the avenging husband, the young lovers caught in their nightshirts in the glare of a policeman's flashlight. Then, as the house falls in darkness again, stop a moment and see the poets, as verse deserts them in the violence of their love. The moon rises above a dingy London street, where the handsome young man lives who possesses only a black-dyed corduroy jacket and five socks, three with holes in them. Then the moon swings around to meet the dawn. And still they bite and kiss.

He sees in her a river in the North, where salmon leap through white water to reach a clear pool.

He sees a Cadillac, a long straight road, a gas station, and a murder, with plains stretching like paper to the horizon, written over with small farms like confessions on an unending scroll. He sees mountains and torrents in the untamed acres of America.

And he pulls back her hair, takes her by the neck so that the whole vast continent is in his grip.

Then, as her hair swings back, he sees the scar.

*   *   *

She sees Jack and the beanstalk and the giant all in one. She climbs the length of a body so tall and strong that it can uphold the world.

She sees a mouse. She stamps, and brings down her shovel—bam!—as it scurries away into a corner, terrified of her freedom, her candour, her open American face.

She hears his whisper, and translates it into a waterfall roar. Once in the pool and drowning, she gives up the struggle to climb out.

Then, as she sees his eyes on the insignia of her death, the scar high on her cheek of her three-year-old suicide attempt, she sees her father come in the door.

*   *   *

He sees her freeze, her eyes pop as the vision strangles her and won't let go. And he brings her to the ground. It hurts: it's rape! But he sees her eyes still straining there, at the dirty corner of the filthy room.

Now he sees America strung with barbed

wire: Keep Out!

But it's too late. They're entwined and they can't escape. They can no longer see each other, or themselves, or the grey day below the fading moon at the window pane.

All they can see is the ghost of Otto, as it grows stronger in the light of day.

Water

Cambridge, England, 1956

England has arteries that are clogged with a green weed, in May. Water lilies, small and wild, lie in chains along the water's surface and lure bright-eyed girls from punts to fall Ophelia-like to the river's muddy bottom. Cuckoos call; hawthorn (unlucky to bring indoors) is red and white along the banks. Ted pushes the boat under a willow tree and he and Sylvia lie half hidden, and read and kiss. They're happy. There can be this spring only once in a lifetime. It is May.

None of this stops Ted's poems from going out, typed and then addressed in Sylvia's American hand, as round as her smiling face. They go across an ocean Ted has never crossed, to publishers of books and magazines, to obscure organs and popular journals, and to poetry competitions that Sylvia knows he has to win. Men come first, in this spring of a world where women in their aprons sprinkle flour, sift icing sugar, and, like Sylvia, dream of all-American kitchens in which to bake the longed-for cookies and pies. It is right that men should come first—so Sylvia believes, as she lies dreaming in a bower of buttercups and clover, where water seeps up against overgrown grasses on the riverbank and then oozes away in gentle waves when another courting couple comes by. Men come first; she will be happy to take second place.

Sylvia can't help admiring this creature from the deep she's landed in spite of herself. In spite of having been so recently in love with Richard, and with Philip—in spite of her own plunges into despair and sudden reachings for the heights—she knows she has him. She knows, too, that the beauty of the man who lies like an athlete resting in the stern means that women will flock to him; but, for now, she admires him—and herself—simply for the masterful ease with which she pulled him in. It was as if Ted, this giant among men, had been waiting to be caught.

Of course, Sylvia fears her own naïveté. She'll lose him one day—but no, she's stopped thinking that, even. Her mother, Aurelia, is told of the coming into Sylvia's life of a paragon of strength and total reliability. And Sylvia has come to give credence to her own letters home.

Everything that Ted loves seems to come from water. When he strides across meadows purple with clover and bee orchid, his thoughts are fixed on salmon, as they lie in his mind's eye on the river bed, dappled as the pebbles that lie under the clear water. When he comes to visit Sylvia he brings shrimps, rosy as a baby's fingernail, that bring the great flat waste, the dredging nets of Camber Sands, into thought and then to a declamation: 'I want to take you to the sea.' But Ted knows—and somewhere Sylvia knows (but she takes pains to conceal the knowledge)—that America's seas are finer and freer than anything to be found in this neat land with its forest of prohibiting notices. Where in England are the paths down to the beaches where no one can be seen? It's better to stay on canals and rivers here, and paddle through congesting weed.

Today Ted arrives from Tenison Road at Sylvia's room with an air of triumph. They'll have a good supper tonight, after all. They're as poor as beggars in a fairy tale—and, as in a fairy tale, kind nature has been sure to provide. A trout hangs from Ted's trouser pocket and he smells of pond slime as he kisses her. Held in the spell of water, Ted and Sylvia set the pan over the gas ring and slide in his catch. How happy they are!—and so they tell each other as they sit long over their feast and pick bones from the fish's delicately tinted flesh.

The Wedding

It's hard for Ted to take no for an answer.
He's seen the wedding, it's as clear as a dream,
and like a dream it moves smoothly, but with
no respect for time or geography through its
paces. The bride: he'll take her hand when
they leave the altar and he'll guide her down
the royal red carpet to the waiting crowds. But
the choir is only just arriving—and the bridal
couple are surrounded by white-ruffed,
scarlet-gowned birds, fluttering and flying and
landing on the flagstones of a great square in
Venice. A river glints beyond, with a barge
waiting. Then Sylvia's mother comes forward,
smiling, nervous—and he's back in front of the
vicar again, who explains that the couple can't
marry in Westminster Abbey however much
the groom may want it. The local church is St
George's—won't that do? And, of course, the
handsome man in the dyed black corduroy
jacket has to say it will.

For nights after, Ted dreams of the jewels
Sylvia will wear on the great occasion. Rubies
gleam in the sun as the bells of the Abbey ring
out; diamonds—as bright as water—hang
around her neck, festooned with emeralds like
weeds. On her head the bride wears a tiara—
but here, satisfied with the richness of his

52

dream, Ted usually wakes. He knows he's bound for fame, for the throne of a king. The Abbey will take him one day, that's for sure.

The actual event is so empty of ritual, of the symbolism he needs to feel himself master of a world of his own making, that Ted is in another kind of dream, a daydream, as he stands without even a best man or a witness—there's only the sexton to hand him the ring—next to a new wife in a pink knitted dress.

His dream at the marriage is more diurnal, fragmented: this, the sixteenth of June, is the day of James Joyce, of Molly Bloom. He sees the ordinary day, the ceremony that lacks any ceremonial, with the fervour of his hero. He sees a pint of Guinness and the workaday faces of the people in the pubs where they'll go to celebrate. He sees himself and his beautiful brown-eyed wife as part of a crowd, lovers with no name, a bride and groom whose only traces will be their signatures in the musty-smelling book down in the crypt, where the pages are eaten through by silverfish.

But as he walks from the empty church, past the blowing paper bags and dogs' turds on the pavement—and smiles at a woman hurrying past who sees Sylvia in her pink dress as a bride and stops, frowns, then smiles—as he leads the new Englishwoman Sylvia has become to her fixture and to her fate, Ted knows that their traces will be monumental, terrifying. He pauses a second, as if waiting for

53

the photograph that doesn't come. Then, unrecorded, smiling at each other as if they could never stop, the newly married couple walks on.

Honeymoon, Benidorm, July 1956

There is something wrong, a wrongness that lies dormant, like the rats that scuttle in the rafters overhead at Widow Mangada's, on an endless treadmill of bad dreams: quiet all day, feverish as Sylvia's racing brain all night.

What is it? There is a silence and heaviness in Ted, who will sit an hour on the hillside, playing God with a colony of red ants. There is a raucousness in Sylvia, which fights his thick-fingered, slow-witted games. 'I hate it here,' she says; and he turns to look at her. A child's toy harbour lies behind him in the glint of turquoise sea, and he smiles up at the woman who is as gaunt as a scarecrow against the sun. 'The Widow Mangada tried to poison us last night'—even as Sylvia speaks, she hears the hysteria, the madness, in her voice. She, the tall woman, the Americana, should not succumb to the powers of the widow, the curse of the faulty gas burner, the dry screech of a waterless tap. What is wrong, what is the matter?

But a man must show his wholeness, a man cannot wax or wane as his wife does, a man as round and constant and burning as the

54

dreadful sun kneels still on the bare, red Spanish soil and has no reply for her. The ants perform miracles, to escape the labyrinth he has constructed for them. He rises, and goes over to take her by the hand. 'We're not poisoned,' he says, and his voice is low; there is no hint of mockery there. Doesn't Ted believe that his new bride can summon anything from the darkness he already knows to his cost is always with her? 'If Widow Mangada wished us to die,' he goes on, still as serious as if he were explaining a scientific problem to a young student, 'then we'd be dead by now.'

Sylvia doesn't laugh: she doesn't know how to mock herself, for life at home and school, life with a mother who will push, push, push, is deadly serious. So she mistakes Ted's tone for one of reproach, and strides away, calling after her, 'It bubbled, you heard it bubble . . . She threw in magic powders . . . She wills us to die.'

And this time a thud of feet on the scorched earth of the hill, a hand on her shoulder, a great bellow of a laugh that wakes her into love again, like a trumpet call. 'It's bicarbonate of soda,' Ted shouts against the dry wind that rises from a sea as wrinkled and bright as a sheet of plastic, festooned with tiny boats. 'That's all she was doing, throwing in the salts . . .' And they both laugh at last, fall and then roll through the prickly shrub, heaving with laughter until they reach the grassless stretch above the road. Death, for a minute or

55

so at least, has lost them: like the red ants in the deserted colony up above, they are out of its clutches, ferrying morsels of everyday life in this landscape where there is nowhere to hide. 'Fresh sardines for supper,' Sylvia sings out as she climbs into the rented car foolishly left exposed in the oven of the Spanish afternoon. 'Pans of cold water,' comes the answer as they accelerate along the road, the little car squeaking at the bends, in the race for air to cool the impossible heat. They aim for tonight's feast: the wine, the lovemaking, the seizing of the present, the triumph of now over the imponderable, ever-impending hour of death. What in Spain has exacerbated in both of them the longing for and dread of annihilation? Why does the sense of wrongness, thrown flippantly from the window of a moving car, return with their arrival at the widow's house? It stays as they walk down the pebbled path, past the vines, and up to the first-floor room with its French windows and all the Mediterranean touches described so carefully by Sylvia in her drafts for stories and her letters home. What is it? It lingers on the landing like the smell of blood.

*   *   *

Spain is red, and Sylvia's skin burns, her white skin in the red dust of the bullring is flushed and blotched by the sun's kisses. She hates

Spain, she hates the blood as it mounts in her, excited by the coming of her time, and prepares to spurt fresh as the wounds of the goaded bull. Ted likes to see the goring, fighting, dying, of the beast as young women in the stadium stamp and hiss and clap. To Sylvia, as she watches the ancient, cruel sport, a faintness comes and then a rage that brings a redness behind the eyes, a blistering of the face, a pain like a stabbing in the gut. Like the bull in its last lunge toward the scarlet cape, she falls on the man she married and tugs his arm. 'I want to go, we must both go'—as if the indignity, the mortification, of being witness to this last, heaving death cannot be theirs to share. 'No—you go,' he mutters, lost in the blare of music, the stench of animal defeat. And she sickens, knowing that in his knowingness he blames her own bleeding for her squeamish wish to flee. Her blood speaks for her: she is her blood: it pours from her while the bull's bright wounds, red eyes opening and closing in its sleek, dead hide, blink up at her like signals.

Later, Sylvia sobs as she searches for water in the old witch Mangada's house. Clean, clear water is all she wants—and it is locked away from her by the old woman, whose paying guests are unable to wash or make coffee in this insane boarding-house. Is Sylvia herself mad? Is she ruled by the moon, as she sometimes feels she must be—barren, ripening in the pale mornings, and then pomegranate—full to bursting with her unborn seed? Will she die without ever giving birth? How many children has she murdered, in those periodic torrents of blood?

For Sylvia knows she is pulled by a stronger tide than most women. She is high and dry when the tide is out, half-dead on shingle that has no memory of the lapping waves. Then, borne on the incoming flood, she tosses like flotsam with the moods, the changes, and the tantrums of pools and hidden reefs, till finally she plunges, losing consciousness as she dives. When she is recovered from the sea, her cheeks are scratched and her nose itches in the intolerable coming of the blood. This is what she must bear, it is why she plays her games with the moon and hates her husband for his pretence of sameness, his stolid mask—while beneath it all another planet holds him prisoner, a planet as fixed as Saturn, as punitive and cold as death.

To the North

Yorkshire, Autumn 1956

What a strange country this is, with its placid streams and outgrown hamlets, and spires like sharpened pencils reaching up to a white sky!

How could this have been the land that inspired the great poets?—and Ted too, for he will be numbered among them, Sylvia has little doubt about that. How could something so small, so apparently insignificant, as England produce all this self-confident genius?

The answer—as far as the man who sits back in the grimy carriage, oblivious to discomfort, landscape, temperature, is concerned —begins to make itself apparent as the satanic horrors of the Midlands recede and lakes and moors appear. There's even a satisfying storm: quickly over but dramatic, even frightening, as hills and turns darken, and the bracken, miles of hostile, dead-brown bracken, goes a deep orange in the play of sun, hail, and rain. This is the country of Wordsworth, the landscape of the Romantics! For a while, as Sylvia sits staring out the sooty window of the antiquated train, she is satisfied she has the answer to the nature of the man she has married in haste and loves more, understands less, each day. Chasms fall away as the engine pushes painfully upward; valleys where no man, or so she likes to believe, has ever gone open up before her. It's wonderful! But a part of Sylvia knows that it's nothing compared to America. Wherever she goes in this minuscule land still constrained by post-war regulations and prohibitions, she finds that she thinks with longing of prairies, deserts, and canyons she has never even seen.

Ted's parents are as hard to fathom as the craggy country they seem happy in—or indifferent to, at least. The house is snug and warm. But Sylvia can't help noticing her new mother-in-law's quick, curious glances at the girl who allowed the younger son of the family to marry (so it feels, anyway) without inviting his own parents to the wedding. Secrecy—the older woman's brow knots when they try to explain the need to keep the fact of their marriage quiet, for fear of Sylvia's college finding out and banishing her from Cambridge. Secrecy—it appears to be a foreign concept to the mother who bustles in the kitchen now. (Such a primitive kitchen, Sylvia thinks, and is reminded of her poor facilities in Eltisley Avenue and then of her own mother's gleaming conveniences, only to be consumed by a wave of homesickness.)

Ted has the air of one who left home long ago and never really returned, sending instead of himself a facsimile: bluff, good-natured, and utterly alien. His hair, Sylvia notices not for the first time, has recently been cut in a pudding-bowl shape—if he weren't so godlike (he is to her and becomes greater in stature the more she is with him), he could be thought a short-spoken, ill-mannered soldier. (The bluffness, to Sylvia, is tantamount to rudeness, but the father and mother give every sign of being satisfied with this stranger who has come into their home.)

Chintz; a coal fire; lamps that give Sylvia a headache with their coloured shades. She feels herself even more removed than the stubborn, silent man her husband has become. Panic begins, with a lurch and a high rushing in the ears; her face pales: all the symptoms Ted can steer her from when they're alone together at home. Sylvia has to be the one to find a place she can lock herself away; and to say, into kind but puzzled faces: 'I would so love a bath!'

*　　*　　*

How long the days are here, with the clock ticking in the kitchen and scones going into and coming out of the oven, and the sound of the father's steps trudging over linoleum to the door, then back again as if an escape had been tried only to be abandoned straightaway. How different their home is from the hills outside in their shifting pillars of mist, growing and falling away with each change in the light. Is all this cosiness a protection against the wildness of the moors, or the sense—at once picked up by Sylvia—of death from TB, of the Brontës in their terrifying parsonage set right up against the graves, of a cruelty of climate and terrain that never could be found in the South? Or is Sylvia, as she runs after the countryman who is now her husband—tripping on sharp stones hidden under spiky tufts of grass, splashing across mountain streams deeper than the brown water will at first admit—is Sylvia afraid of her own loneliness to come, and inventing hostility on the part of her new parents-in-law? Does she see herself abandoned?—as Ted abandons her now, but only with the stride of a man so accustomed to this unwelcoming land that he's absentminded rather than deliberately neglectful of his wife. How is it, the faster he covers ground, the more determined Sylvia is to catch up with him?

It's the day when rain comes down like a great head of hair hanging over the flanks of the hill, a giant's head with rolling eyes that are treacherous pools in bog and black stubble, cheeks where heather burned in the last creeping fire. The day Sylvia won't forget; yet neither the father nor mother think anything of it when later, trembling and shaking, the strange American girl stumbles back into the house. It's the day Ted killed the deer.

Sylvia has tried not to see this man—whose nerve endings, heartbeat, thoughts, and dreams match hers—as a killer. But she knows by now that he cannot walk across this land without the knowledge of where his next victim may lie: rook, pigeon, rabbit, hare. She has seen him lift the gun as if it's no more than another limb, to point out to her a cairn, a fairy ring set in sphagnum moss that's eerie emerald green. But it is a gun. The sickening thump of falling bird haunts her at night as she lies under the padded quilt in the stifling room. Ted kills, and he loves to kill.

The deer—Sylvia hardly sees it before it's down, falling near its young, who scatter at the muffled sound of the shot, in this foggy mouth of the giant's cavern in the hill. She stares in terror, then in disgust, at the grace and beauty of the slaughtered animal; and, for the first time, she sees the man she married as hideous, obscene.

'We'll have a stew tonight,' this man says, and she sees from the elation that brings a glow to his face that he is hungry, greedy for the tastes of his kill. 'I'll show you the best way to cook it, if you like.'

'It's pitiful!' And he sees the anger in the woman who is foreign to him in her rage and her understanding of her rage—for she is no Englishwoman, despite the submissiveness, the yearning to be docile she so often weeps for. Sylvia is American: she will speak out. 'I'm going—' She turns from the scene: Ted, with his gun slung over his arm, the deer hidden on boggy land, under a bed of reeds. She strides, unhesitating, across the treacherous terrain, turns once, and shouts into a fine drizzle, a mist that shrouds his still, uncomprehending form: 'What is to be done?'

Ouija

How do you discover if someone loves you? How can you find your story when all the filaments are there, and the bright light of good intention—but you simply don't yet know what it can be? At twenty-four, do you fear there will never be a story, and life will go on, as dull as an unlit lamp?

There's only one answer to those questions and it comes from the ether, the world beyond, the world of Yeats and his scribbling, spirit-conscious wife. If Georgie could do it, Sylvia can: she'll be poet and muse both; she'll take dictation from the ghosts of centuries long gone. She'll train as an astrologer and buy a crystal ball.

Ted is the one who's seen deep into this woman he suspects of genius, of striving to reach the stars without a ladder or a compass to guide her there. He knows he can help Sylvia, with his talent with the tarot cards and his study of occult powers. He takes it all seriously, and soon she does too. After all, coincidences and correspondences are drawn as if magnetically to Ted. Where does his magic spring from? Like a hero of the ancient world, he reaffirms the possibility of superhuman status, conferred by the gods at birth. If Ted believes this 'mumbo jumbo', as most of his friends consider it to be, then Sylvia must follow the horoscopes, the sign charts, the I Ching too. The only unfortunate detail is that in their sessions with a homemade ouija board there comes a visitant whose name is actually Jumbo. Who is having on whom, in this cramped first-floor flat in cold, prosaic Cambridge?

Sylvia doesn't care if people laugh or stare when she speaks of her new obsession. Like a proud housewife preparing a meal for husband, faculty members, professors of the austere colleges in their city, she lays out the new tools of her otherworldly trade. A brandy glass, polished until it shines, shows her face bulbous in reflection as she sets it on the coffee table. Letters of the alphabet, cut from sketching paper, surround the glass. There! She is ready, in the laboratory of spells and mysteries, questions and answers, that 55 Eltisley Avenue has become. No matter that she and her Herculean husband, brought to a level neither likes by poverty (despite hard work and discipline), have to share the only bathroom in the house with another couple, he a man Sylvia once had loved. They can transcend primitive conditions and demeaning reminders of dead passions. The ouija board will transport them to the truths and certainties of another world.

Tonight is a vile night, with a bitter wind blowing in from the fens. The comfort, sophistication, and glory of Sylvia's homeland seems far away. 'Dinge!' say friends, all brought up to bear the privations of an England still devastated by the effects of war and shortages of food, luxury, anything to lift the spirits and bring on a smile. 'Dinge,' they say, and they mean the antiquated plumbing, sad little restaurants that serve uneatable food, clothes in windows that look as if they're modelled by dead women: dateless, lost to fashion, dim.

No one appears to realise the efforts Sylvia must make to escape the all-pervading depression—hers, the climate's, the smug indifferent colleges', with their fine architecture and disapproving glares. Some who call, perhaps, see the bright dance of letters around the upturned glass as a gesture of defiance to logic, to the Cambridge insistence on the rational mind. Others think she's simply barmy. Oddly, Ted is spared the judgment of those who come to the first-floor flat on Eltisley Avenue. His fate and future fame are written all over him. Sylvia it is who has to put up with the scorn and sarcasm of the visiting friends. But there aren't all that many of these. And tonight, as she goes to draw the worn red velour curtains against the poking, interfering wind, there's no risk of anyone coming here at all.

Ted and Sylvia sit in a dim light, just bright enough to see the capital letters where the balloon glass stops before swooping and skittering on across the coffee table. They've called up a drowned seaman; then there's the maiden aunt of a Victorian medium; now, at last, comes the most faithful of the visitors they have come to prefer to the dreary dinge-merchants, academics and their gawking wives, who inhabit Cambridge. Pan has come. If the wind howls in the chimney (converted to a miserable gas fire), there may arrive his successor, the spirit with news of Prince Otto, royally named in the underworld and indubitably the twelve-years-dead father of Sylvia.

Pan guides the glass, which rustles and squeaks on the imitation wood like a dancing matron, full-bodied and round-cheeked. Pan has news of an imperial past: Sylvia's mind empurples, she lies half in a trance in a bower of vines heavy with black grapes. Wherever she came from, wherever she may one day belong, it will never be to small-minded Cambridge. Yet she writes well here: the ouija board leads her into words and rhythms that are more truly her own than any she has written so far. Some would say, doubtless, that her husband of less than four seasons is really the one responsible for poems accepted by respected journals; that his is the finger that shoves round the glass. Sylvia is ready for this; she is certainly no fool.

Of course it's our subconscious minds steering, she says with a smile. And some say it's the heat from our bodies that propels the glass around. And she and Ted exchange glances and laugh.

*　　　*　　　*

Ted and Sylvia are going to America, to teach, to learn (in Ted's case) the manners of this lovely, smooth country where—as he believes —shark-finned cars cruise slowly down the streets, and gleam and grin; and children are allowed everything they ask for.

There's something childish about Ted, so Sylvia thinks sometimes as she sees him sitting over the makeshift oracle, their mirror into the future, with its upturned glass and flame of cardboard letters. Does he really think his wishes will be granted if he asks 'Pan' or 'Jumbo' to fulfil them? And why does he dwell so long on death, on messages from her long-dead father, Otto? It's as if he foresees his own fame, and her descent into the grave, his accolades and praise followed by the long dark silence he almost appears to want to guide her down, a path where no one knows her poems or her name. 'You're ambitious,' Ted says, smiling at her one day when work sent out has been returned to her, when grim depression comes in the humble low-ceilinged room and takes her by the throat. 'Your mother's ambition has passed down to you. Your father waits—he's here now—listen!' And she leans her head sideways, persuaded as always by the lovely voice and the tenderness that veils the mockery, never far away. 'He has your story, listen to what he says.'

But on days like this, Sylvia can hear nothing. Clever as she is, she cannot imagine that this still-new, loving husband would poison the well of their own making, turn the spotlight in his own direction, and leave her stranded in this country it's so hard to understand or love. Yet when he tells her that one of them must die, and gives a great laugh at the punch line—'There's not room enough for both of us in the world'—she feels a languor, a giving-in to death, to the father Ted tells her she loves more than she cares for him. She feels a heavy-limbed longing for the sacrifice of suicide: Ted was born to conquer and she is bereft of even the desire for life. He'll do so well without her! She sees him entertaining important men, he is the embodiment of hospitality. Without her, he has every right to walk and sleep with blonde-haired girls.

Today, Ted teaches Sylvia the art of memory. She closes her eyes and sees the Roman columns he word-paints for her; and she hears the voices of orators as they place each clause on its appointed pillar, and drive long, impassioned speeches deep into their minds. 'It's like this,' Ted says, kissing her awake again, half-hypnotised: 'Here'—he points to the screen, scruffy, orange velvet with drooping medallions of dust—'Place your first stanza here'—and he strides triumphantly around the tiny room—'and the next here'. Sylvia stares, her poem flying to attach itself to the standard lamp, hideous in its post-war British parchment shade, which dominates the dark corner of the room. 'Now, speak it!'—and she does, laughing, amazed, as the columns of Rome bring back her words to her, in the unlikely surroundings of a suburban house.

*   *   *

Their fingers rest once more on the glass balloon but the voices won't come through. There is packing to do, a visit to friends in Cambridge before the long journey across an ocean Ted cannot see even in his mind's eye. The concentration isn't there, though 'Otto' said last night they'd be lost far out in the water and find themselves stranded on a rock where mussels cling, going under at high tide. (Ted laughed this one off—then gravely, teasing, said to Sylvia that this meant she'd join her father as she longed to do, and for a marriage present the dead man would give her the molluscs' pearls for eyes.) 'There's no one here tonight,' Ted says, and yawns. He pulls a sweater knitted by his mother from behind his

70

chair and puts it on.

As Ted goes to his pals—'I'll have a word with them first, see you in an hour or so'— Sylvia stays quite still and desolate in this room that will by tomorrow no longer be her home. Yes—she wants fame!—she sees it some days as a story for the 'slicks', magazines where success is measured in feather boas and homes in the Hamptons and long, slinky legs in sheer silk. At other times she yearns for the admiration of the poets she emulates and admires: Theodore Roethke, Marianne Moore, and her new idol, Robert Lowell. But she knows now that she will never attain fame, however much she may crave it. She knows that kind Ted is right: for Sylvia is damaged and he is not: she lost her innocence when she gained the scar, while Ted, shooting skyward every day with his new poems, is touched only by the fire of inspiration. Sylvia's sole surviving poem will be the ballad of the dead Otto as he rises shining from the sea.

*   *   *

And, as neither Sylvia nor her fondly greeted husband in this new land is surprised to discover, a good portion of Otto's prophecy comes true. It's more that Sylvia greets the drifting boat carrying them to a half-submerged reef, out at Cape Cod, with a kind of fatal acceptance, meek and hostile, bitter

71

and almost satisfied with the actions of the gods in taking them so young; while Ted, exclaiming at the beauty of the schools of fish they glide over on this windless day, lives right to the last: fearless, strong.

They're rescued. There are no mussels on the bare reef and it does not serve as a launch-pad to the submarine hell of Otto Plath. It's all over in half a day, actually. But death is always seen and seized on—whether lurking in an insect that flies in at night, or coming straight out of the blue, like today's near-fatal accident, boat and stranded passengers as plain and brightly coloured as a drawing by a child. Death is always there, for Ted; and so he brings it back to Sylvia. Neither needs reminding that she's the one who had gone so far as to swallow the contents of a bottle with fifty pills.

America, 1957–59

Electra

What has the mother done wrong, to deserve the avenging hatred of her daughter? In gated walls where Sylvia's death-shrieks, prehistoric in their sure knowledge of disaster, sound each night at sunset, is there written no explanation of the crime? A silent burial bell of stone contains the betraying mother, two and a half thousand years dead beneath a lintel guarded by a regiment of bees. No one can give the nature of the misdemeanour of Aurelia Plath. There hasn't even been a foppish lover to spring on unawares and drown in the nets of Sylvia's fury and scorn.

Yet Aurelia appears to know nothing of this as she serves the drinks in the backyard at Wellesley. A wedding party!—a second, real celebration, to mark the marriage of dear Sivvy to the most handsome, kind-hearted man, already a poet of repute, steady and calm, a perfect antidote to Sylvia's too-frequent hysteria. Is it the fear of her mother's welcome of him as a panacea for her ills—a man, after all, indubitably a sensible and therefore always-right member of the sex Sylvia dreads and loves—is it a fear of Mrs Plath's instant recognition of the superiority of Ted that drives the daggers into Sylvia's heart? Or does she, with the incestuous envy of a daughter of the House of Atreus, sicken and thrill at the sight of the woman she first loved—then, with the going of the father, grew to hate—without a man? Clytemnestra of the canapés and iced drinks, veiled killer who excels in the polite and professional chitchat expected of an intelligent teacher—does Sylvia actually suspect the husband she has brought here to America of having been accepted by Aurelia as a substitute for Otto? The bees

73

drone by the low door to the death chamber where her mother, resplendent in gold and robes of purple, lies indestructible in her unplundered tomb. A hand reaches out—the new husband steps in to lie beside her, and both grin, to the accompaniment of bees.

Sylvia will teach at Smith, and she will write, and she'll glimpse the golden-haired girls Ted walks with in their Bermuda shorts and pageboy bobs. But Sylvia's pageboy makes her seem just that—an eager server, plain as the halfgrown scion of a family anxious to ingratiate itself at court—while the girls she sees Ted with are glamorous behind their swinging hair. Sylvia is trapped in a court where Ted and Aurelia, king and queen, play out the ancient tragedy. Her husband, whom she must see and touch a hundred times a day to feel herself real, to be reminded of the nature of reality, is Claudius to her Hamlet, murderer of the true king.

Smith, in fact, is the court where Sylvia, tense with nerves, must hold her own. Adulteries in the English department crackle in the play-within-a-play that is academic life. The department chairman has married girls from Smith—one after the other, naturally— but Sylvia dreams at night of multiple death-weddings, maimed corpses in their bridal attire—and Ted, caught by the lures of pageboy blondes, at an altar that transforms, halfway through, into his grave.

There's nothing to do but to go and visit Otto himself, or this illness will grow more monstrous still. Why can't Aurelia see it? Sylvia begins, as paranoia throttles with its ivy grip, to imagine husband and mother in a deadly plot, a conspiracy to drive her mad. In the torture chambers where she walks in her night-long insomnia, the woman who has sacrificed everything for her daughter—and the man who gives all his care and attention, sole witness of her poetry and her madness, to his wife—prepare their instruments with gloating care. Red-hot needles gouge out her eyes. An arm is snapped with a mere dancing movement of the beautiful stranger's wrist. Those who love Sylvia are, she knows, those who desire to do her harm.

But who exactly is this calm and steady man, this ideal son-in-law for lonely mothers everywhere? What games does he play when he guides an impressionable young woman to her father's burial plot? Hasn't he already ensured his total mastery of the dead man's daughter? Gold chains swing before her eyes; and the orb, as it goes back and forth in the dull, small apartment in Northampton where they live, dictates the poems and the nightmares too. Breathe!—and she inhales, a long breath that will carry her to childhood, to the empty beach, a tide racing in, where she was dispatched at the time both of her baby brother's birth and of Otto's death. He tells

75

her that this is the path to the very centre of her being and her consciousness: Breathe! But Sylvia finds no beginning here, only a sense of loss that makes her beg him to stop. For the path takes her nowhere. It's merely Azalea Path, the least visited and most important grave site in the world.

You could say that Aurelia knows nothing of this side of the man Sylvia dreams of as her mother's husband and her own missing father, the man who has risen from the meek, overcrowded cemetery to take Prince Otto's place. Aurelia doesn't know the tarot cards; or the book on witches—she glimpsed it once, at a picnic, but Ted snatched it back from her, Sylvia glowering at him as if possessed herself. How can her admired new son-in-law, a normal, sane man with an interesting future, be mixed up with these discreditable things? So Aurelia looks away. She puts it all from her mind. The man who came across the Atlantic from ordered Cambridge (Aurelia can't take in the Yorkshire moors, for all that Sylvia wrote and spoke of Emily Brontë and was herself at Wuthering Heights: Aurelia knows only that Cambridge is the natural home of Ted)—this paragon of steadiness and calm could surely not be mired in a medieval past of devils and demons from the deep?

But he is; and he has pulled Sylvia in with him. A perfect husband, to lead her to the place where Otto lies buried, on Azalea Path.

76

*   *   *

What does Ted think of as he follows his wife from the grave with its pink marble slab and the plastic flowers she says grow straight from her dead father's navel? How does he comfort this strange woman who lives, since her descent into the first suicide, the Hades of the cinder blocks under her mother's house, half the time, by her own admission, in the winter of depression and despair and the other half summer—gay, complacent, content? He knows—so he tells those who wonder at their symbiotic relationship—each thought that flickers through Sylvia's mind, before it's either discarded or made electric by its conjunction with new thoughts and words. Each can feel what the other thinks, without having to exchange information. But are they happy, people ask. And today, as he stands and sees her cry her heart out by the mean gravel patch, he must wonder if they are or ever can be.

The world is more Sylvia's domain, for all the accusations of self-absorption and a solipsistic nature, than it can ever be Ted's. It is Sylvia who flames in rage at the segregation in schools in the South, in Arkansas; Sylvia who champions the bus campaigns, supports the struggle for the integration of black children. It is she who hates all that

77

Eisenhower stands for—and begs her mother (Ike has had a serious heart attack) not to vote for Nixon if the president has to leave office. She sees America with a cold, dispassionate eye: imperialist power in the invasion of Lebanon and the threat of war in China over Chiang Kaishek; corruption in the scandal of the vicuna coat, taken as a bribe by Eisenhower's chief of staff. And she knows herself alone, as far as those near to her are concerned, in these opinions, for neither Ted nor Aurelia expresses the slightest dissatisfaction with things as they are. Sylvia and her rages at the land she belongs to, the land that is the most powerful in the world, can be—and frequently are—marked down to the general malaise from which the poor, brilliant girl has always suffered. In short, when Sylvia fumes, she's mad. It's true that she's self-absorbed, indeed she is; and it probably occurs to her very little to wonder what Ted sees in America. Or perhaps she fears he's enamoured of the movie image, and of the verse and songs that pulse through the nation. The sheer freedom of the million highways and railroads that crisscross this giant of a country like lines across a fossil, markings of lost journeys, of the new geology of the age, hold him as spellbound as a child. Here, as he says with great relish, 'you can travel forever and no one knows where you are'. And Sylvia looks at him fearfully, and then away again. For Ted likes more and more to go where he is undiscovered: to meet the pageboy girls, as she believes, with no one guessing where he may be.

Rage

A story of a rosebud and an armful of blossoms from a rose tree: of a walk in a park at dusk and the rage Sylvia feels for the three girls who emerge from a clump of rhododendron bushes, their bounty held triumphantly aloft. Why—as she asks herself in her journal, and then in a poem—why shouldn't the girls help themselves to the flowers, when she and Ted steal a rose every few days from this very place, Child's Park, to savour the fragrance in a wineglass of water each morning when they wake?

She feels terror at her rage. She wants to kill them. But the girls, younger and happier than herself, more innocent in their pleasures and ambitions, have unknowingly desecrated holy ground. Nothing grows under rhododendrons: dead land spreads from the roots of these Himalayan trees and poisons neighbouring plants. Grass doesn't grow. No animal can live there.The stately, elegant rhododendron kills. And the sole shrub that will grow in its vicinity is the azalea.

Paradise Pond

Sylvia teaches; Ted glows in the fame that was born with him and rests, Janus-faced, on his shoulder: he knows the good fame now and has already a suspicion of the evil fame that one day will turn to face the world. He's prodigal with his gifts; the scraps of paper that fall from his desk burn with his discarded words; and his appetites are Rabelaisian. He's a giant when he eats, Falstaff when he quaffs the wine Sylvia watches nervously, fearful of the money running out, and her husband's luck and fame as well. His poems are beginning to become as celebrated as the man they call 'Ted Huge', the man who eclipses his teacher wife and strides around the provincial confines of Smith College and Northampton, a lion escaped from the boredom and constrictions of a minor zoo.

Now the husband-and-wife team—a team that is increasingly a one-man show—will go to Boston for a house party. They'll make plans to move there when this year's final semester has passed; they dream, both, of the real lions they'll meet and sup with once they're on Beacon Hill. Robert Lowell, admired by Sylvia, has a poetry workshop at Harvard. This coming weekend Ted will read there, to the growing band of people who see him as one of the great talents of the future. Sylvia, unhappy and resentful, will hear him as if from miles away: poems she typed out, poems she took to the post office, lines she rescued from the pen of a man who must be cleaned for, cleaned up after, fed. The poems mean only these chores to her now; and as his voice rings out and people join in the applause, she sees the soapsuds in the bowl, the vacuum cleaner when it disgorges his rubbish at the end of another enervating day. Why can't she write? When she says that nothing comes—when she blames herself, as all writers do—she sees only the statue of a successful writer, only Ted. The self-contained, uncomprehending stone effigy of a man she loves but—now, more and more and in place of herself—blames, blames, blames.

A child will make all the difference. But anything Sylvia sets her mind on, she thinks in this bitter mood, will be denied her. She's barren!—of course she must be. The moon draws out her entrails, month by month. Ted is the fertile one, spewing lines that wrestle and edge against one another in their race to escape the womb. His whole being is enveloped in a coating of primeval dust: she cleans him, polishes him, berates his filthy fingernails and lank, unwashed hair. Ted emerges each day from the cramped vestibule where his modest table is set up, as triumphant as a woman who has experienced multiple births.

Along with the sense of emptiness, of a mind fighting through the exercises and subjects suggested by the man who comes taller from his cubby-hole each day Sylvia hears the tolling of the marriage bell: infidelity, betrayal, lies. Why does Ted tell her, in an uncharacteristically hangdog manner, that he doesn't want her at the reading of his friend Paul Roche's translation of *Oedipus* at Smith tonight? He'd rather she didn't come; that's all.

Is it a quarrel that has set Ted against her coming? Didn't she praise him at the Harvard reading and stand as straight as an admiring child in her Alice headband when the poets gathered later to congratulate this new, exciting arrival in their midst? Doesn't Sylvia cook casseroles, potatoes mashed to a fluffy halo to set up above the duck breast for professors, the dessert soufflé for Olive Higgins Prouty when she comes to call? Isn't she the perfect wife? Of all the figs on the groaning tree, hasn't she plucked wifedom, the ripest and the best?

But Ted is adamant. He doesn't want Sylvia to come to Smith, where he will read the part of Creon. He'll come straight home afterward, she can be sure of that. He will, he will.

All night, Sylvia wrestles with what she believes to be his coded message from the ancient world. She dreams herself a child abandoned on a hillside, Oedipus rescued, fatherless as she is, only to meet at the crossing of the roads the man who is her/his father, whom she/he kills.

Does Ted, quite simply, wish to rescue her in turn from the anguish she will feel at the reading when she hears the terrible fate that lies in store for one who kills his father, as she has murdered Otto with her love?

Ted wishes to save her. As Creon, he must give Oedipus to Jocasta, daughter of Laius. Sylvia sweats and pants in the bed where her husband lies so still, as she half-dreams, half-sees her own aversion to the perfumed Jocasta/Aurelia, who must be her spouse, the queen of Thebes.

In the morning, though, it's just the same. Ted refuses to explain or give way. And Sylvia is reduced to childishness again—anything that involves her husband and has echoes of her mother makes her as cunning, duplicitous, and miserable as any kid. Sylvia will find a way in to the auditorium tonight: Sylvia shall find the answer to her sleepless nights.

But the evening is ruined by Sylvia's unwanted appearance in the auditorium. She sees King Creon, reading one minute with all the force and conviction of which her dear Ted is capable—and in the next, as he spots her there up in the back row, he's taken on a funny, furtive voice, gone quiet; the audience begins to cough and get uneasy.

Sylvia feels the panic-bird as it alights on her shoulder and digs its claws deep into her flesh. This stranger, this king who is now an impostor, a petty thief awaiting his captors—she just cannot imagine why the hunted, whispering man at the microphone is acting the way he does.

Then she sees the girl in the front row. The girl is (of course) a pageboy blonde. She sits forward in her seat, her intense, chubby face—Ted would call it a roundy face, Sylvia thinks with fury—beaming up at him like a flower opening to the sun.

This must never happen again. Sylvia trembles with the effort to control herself. She thinks of all the bad things happening in the world, of the wars and tortures that sometimes make her swear she'll never bring children into a world as evil as this one. She thinks of the death of her father and the brave struggle of her mother—all these are important, world-shattering things, and here she is, minding a pageboy blonde in the front row of *Oedipus*. It's infantile, so pathetic that she will impose a strict regimen of study and punishment on herself to ensure that she never suffers for so trivial a cause again.

It makes no difference. However she may try not to, Sylvia shows her rage as they go home, in her clipped, overclear tones and turned-away face. 'No one could hear you,' is all she says to her husband, who still wears the odd, hunted look when they're finally at home. And when she hears him go out into the night, she feels for the first time a great sense of relief.

*   *   *

It's time to leave Smith, and Sylvia and Ted arrange to meet at Paradise Pond before and after her last class. Celebration—a longing for the time in Boston, where the genius she has married will in gratitude to his nearly-as-brilliant wife show his love for her to all the famous poets and writers they'll meet there. Celebration is surely in order, for Sylvia has worked hard at college and has earned enough to keep Ted writing while she taught.

So it's hard to believe that the handsome man (no one could mistake anyone else for Ted) can be seen walking there quite openly with a girl. He'd forgotten the first meeting. Now here he is at Paradise Pond with the girl Sylvia could swear is the owner of the pageboy that gleamed in the borrowed glory of the spotlights at the reading of *Oedipus*. Yes—she looks happily up at him. Her Bermuda shorts are as pink as a tropical sunset. Her breasts lean out of a turquoise blouse knotted provocatively at the waist. How she adores him! How he adores being adored!

Tonight is different from the last time. The fight continues late into the night.

'You're just like your mother,' Ted starts off, knowing the fury that will inflame Sylvia at the accusation: doesn't she sense that her

85

terror and jealousy at seeing him with another woman mirror the desertion her mother suffered at Otto's death?

Sure enough, 'How dare you?' comes from Sylvia, with a kick and a scratching rush at the face seen so recently bathed in a complacent smile. 'I hate you.' And as the tears the mention of hatred always brings—the mother again, the unloving performer of sacrifices on the altar of acceptance and success—begin to pour down her face in earnest, she brushes them away and fights on. Money enters the fight, with the gloves off: it invariably does. Which of them will put their writing into second place, to support the other writer? Not Ted, surely: and Sylvia sees a dead end beckon, when teaching is pushed at her once more as a way to succeed, to earn. They fight; but each knows they have no choice but to win.

Yet . . . isn't she married to the one man who can stand up to her? Doesn't she want a child once she's written poems that will make her famous and a hit novel that will make her rich? Away from the adulterous atmosphere at Smith, a pool bobbing with lust-crazed professors and pageboy blondes, they'll concentrate both on work and on the achievement of fame. They'll find the success Aurelia wants for them.

The Opposite of a Poem

It's April, in a city still cold from the long winter, where the noses of Irish maids as they run out from mansions on wide streets gleam red in chill, cathedral air.

This is the place for doubles, opposites: old Mrs Aldrich, as she comes down the oak staircase to her vast and gloomy dining room, has as her secret sharer a bottle of brandy, concealed in a cupboard designed to contain china and linens; and Robert Lowell, head poking above the crowd of students like an amiable cleric, plays the part of Dr Jekyll half the year and for the next six months he's Hyde.

Boston is forbidding, and so invites misrule. At the Ritz, more and more frequently in this uncertain month, Sylvia can be found at a polished round table with her new friend Anne. They talk of opposites: there's something, as these eager students of Lowell's literature class agree, about the place—and about their own pasts, too—that seems to fall into halves. Plath's life was torn in two by marrying an Englishman (he's here, somewhere, plump-faced and jowly in a photograph with poets and tutors, out of his depth in a foreign land) and she lives in England now, though a good

87

half of her is still permanently embedded in America. Like Anne Sexton, she is a poet—but she is her opposite, as well, for Anne has children and anger and a family concerned at her immense will to create and her growing success. Sylvia is here as Ted's wife, who 'also writes'. She notes her monthly bleeding with dismay. Sylvia wants to be a mother, to feel the love she still believes to be the opposite of pain.

Today they talk—not for the first time—of their attempted suicides. Sylvia's is a parody of the pregnancy she so desires: a craving to crawl back into her mother's womb. She tells of the long hours in the cellar, doped, half-dead, before she is discovered and jolted back into a half-life. Anne, as she waves a hand that's slender, despotic, adorned with a diamond-and-ruby ring, calls for more drinks and says, Oh, for me it is always Nembutal. The Kill-Me-Pills. And they laugh, these semi-goddesses who dare, here in Boston, to follow the advice of their mentor Lowell and spill the beans.

The stingers come. Last week it was martinis, but Anne likes to change her mind: we'll get loaded, let's try stingers this time around. But Sylvia likes the gin: she remembers the little conical lake that was brought to her, an onion like a river pearl lying in its depths, and the pattern of weeds you could see if you looked right through the glass at the waving walls of the Ritz Bar. Anne, peremptory as ever, sends back Sylvia's stinger and demands that it be replaced by a martini— make it large. And they agree, however unlike each other they may prove to be, on one important thing. The free potato chips are essential to their feeling of happiness when they come here. And suicide is, after all, the opposite of a poem, of course it is.

The temptations of both, poetry and suicide, are great, especially when the poet they most revere can alter so radically, shooting from the straight and sensible professor to the fascist playboy, a new blonde each night on his arm when the manic bouts set in. They feel his swings as calls to death that reverberate like Echo's empty answers to the calls of Narcissus. They fear the split in two, the high-octane adrenaline that takes them first a long way from those who love them and then, as if in punishment for their desertion of the good, the outgoing side of their natures abandons them completely, leaves them limp and ready for death. They're on a knife edge here, in this gilt and red-plush and cream-gloss desert island where they meet.

Sylvia would like to talk of her suspicions of Ted's infidelity—certainly he flirts with girl students, but then he's so handsome and strong, why shouldn't he?—but she doesn't, with Anne. Men are too dangerous a subject when the gin sets women confiding, she's heard that hundreds of times before. But her dreams are filled with his going from her. In one dream he kneels before her and confesses he has fallen in love. Sometimes she glimpses the woman he's announced he must now be with: dark, with black eyes and the beauty of a Gypsy or a Byzantine Madonna. Her opposite: her victim and conqueror. But she has to admit she's seen no one here like that.

'More chips, please!' Anne Sexton is waving at a denuded pottery bowl. It's late. A man they hardly know has seen them and is walking up to the table where the women sit. The martini mood departs from Sylvia and she's grumpy and dissatisfied. In the wood of the polished table she sees her face as it looks stonily down at its own reflection. She hates what she sees; she hates herself and most of all she hates her ponytail, swinging now over the dim reflection of her podgy, sweaty face. 'I'll end up just settling for a pageboy cut like I always do,' Sylvia says to Anne as her friend greets the man neither of them really knows. 'I must write a poetry of real situations,' Sylvia says, as the man is now sent to the bar to fetch the chips. 'Behind which the great gods play the drama of blood, lust, and death.'

'Sylvia, do I order you a martini?' the man says, coming up.

'We were talking of opposites,' Anne tells him, and she laughs and lights a cigarette.

'Yes—and of blood, and lust—and our own deaths.'

The North Atlantic, 1960

Slow-slow-quickquick-slow. Assia Gutman lies on her berth, looking out on a rough grey sea and listening to the radio. The foxtrot; the tango; the waltz. She is thirty-two years old and her beauty makes people think of music, if they are sentimentally inclined, or trouble, if they are not. The foxtrot is her especial favourite: she learned the steps in the British officers' club in Tel Aviv, when she was sixteen. Her father, Dr Gutman, is a successful GP with a clinic in Toronto. He and his family were sent visas to Canada when Assia emigrated there with John Steel. Much to the disgust of her sister, Celia, Dr Gutman uprooted his family and went to live near his favourite daughter. Not looking back is an essential component of survival for the Gutmans—and not least for the lovely Assia, who is accompanied on this all-important voyage from Canada to England by her third husband, David. (The first, John, was soon abandoned; the second, Richard, an academic, she left in Vancouver; and now Assia has found a third spouse, who is willing to accompany her back across the ocean, to settle

91

in London.)

What will Assia find there? A student of English literature at Vancouver University, she has spent long enough with the British officers in Tel Aviv and then in her married lives in Canada to have assumed an English accent as well as perfect mastery of the language. But her accent is cut-glass upper-class: a voice that would carry the lovely Mrs Wevill into the smart flats of Knightsbridge more readily than into the portals of the Poetry Society or the company of intellectuals. Its owner, of course, doesn't know this yet.

Assia lies half-dreaming as the liner bears her to the land of Donne and Shakespeare. She listens to the foxtrot and remembers how her silk skirt, excited by the slow-slow-quickquick-slow steps of its high-heeled wearer, rose in a whoosh! to the amusement of other quickstep learners already suffering envy at the sight of so proficient and graceful a dancer as Assia Gutman—Assia smiles as she thinks back on those innocent days. Then, as her husband knocks meekly at the cabin door before coming in, she frowns and leans to pick up the book of poetry that has slid from bunk to floor, Ted Hughes's *Hawk in the Rain*. David Wevill is obsessed with the rising young poet. And Assia writes poetry—it holds, she believes, the secret to her true nature—but like her beauty, it is dark and sad. Both Assia and her Canadian husband hope to be introduced to poets—and if possible, Ted Hughes—once they have settled down to life in London.

Darkness falls and the ship cuts through the waves as grey yet alive with phosphorescence, the hidden electricity of the sea, as the slim-waisted, twirling skirts of many years ago, when Assia Gutman and John Steel together emptied the ballroom floor with one last Charleston or a burst of jive. The rhythm of the ship makes dancers of reclining passengers; knocks pieces from backgammon boards and upsets narrow-stemmed glasses from the steward's hand. The ambition and longing for success and fame of the mysterious and beautiful young woman with the Canadian husband sets the three-piece ensemble playing early, in a cocktail lounge deserted as the seas pile up. Somehow they know that she, the 'other', the one people will see as the swarthy woman of the tarot pack, who comes across water like bad luck, like the Black Death, like a devil, is on board. So what better than to play the tunes and watch her dance?

*   *   *

In October, the month of scarlet leaves at Yaddo, the writers' colony in Saratoga Springs, Sylvia learned she would be having a child. In the artificial quiet, the manufactured 'creative atmosphere' of the park and house in upstate

New York, the making of a new life went on. Poems, obedient to changed rhythms and demands, races and pauses in the bloodstream of their maker, spoke at last more clearly of herself.

There had been a long summer, travelling across America. Then, after Yaddo, came the return to England. But it didn't seem like a return: everything is new. Sylvia's poems are good. When spring comes, a daughter is born and she is beautiful. Apart from the problem of finding somewhere to live, everything is perfect here in London.

The illusion of perfection doesn't last long. For this is the age of 'difficult women' and Sylvia is soon seen by some of Ted's friends as one of the species. She's difficult in refusing offers of bargain beds and sofas and fridges from Dido Merwin: she doesn't want to visit a flea market, buy cheap, and be uncomfortable when she has her baby to care for. This is considered to be difficult. She doesn't want Olwyn, her sister-in-law, coming to stay in the tiny flat on Chalcot Square, preventing her from working and making the quarters more cramped than they already are. She ousts her husband from the study he's been lent to work in and relegates him to the vestibule of the flat. Once Sylvia is placed in the category of 'difficult', there is little warmth shown her. The British, it transpires, are as hard to fathom as their plumbing, which drives poor

Sylvia mad.

How is the day of a woman who is muse and poet, mother and housewife, to contain the gift of a wild animal? How can Ted, tempted by the seller of a fox cub at the underground station, blame a failing marriage on what he knows would be Sylvia's reaction to his bringing the creature home?

But he does. His shirts must be washed and ironed, and the baby cries for food, which Sylvia cooks and mashes (all must be healthy, indeed perfect, here).

His poems must be typed. (Envelopes, stamps, the long trudge to the post office, the queue in London's cold, rainy summer and the tantrums of children waiting there, their mothers wearing the look of smug martyrdom the queuing British love to assume but Sylvia cannot.)

His meals must also be cooked and must include enough for a friend or two. Sylvia is difficult if they're late back from the pub.

There are so many ways of being difficult, as Sylvia discovers. Why, she's even accused of helping herself from a hostess's fridge when she goes with her husband to stay in France. It might be easier, she sometimes thinks, as the brave new life begins to shrink and fade in the light of hostility and disapproval, if she didn't exist at all.

Yet, as ever, she describes herself as radiantly happy; and in some senses she is. She loves her daughter. She writes with power and energy. And finally, as if in answer to her prayers—for space, privacy, rural contentment —a second pregnancy drives the couple to search for a house a long way from London, in the West Country.

England's only offering to the world of a religion was pagan witchcraft. Devon is where Ted and Sylvia find the house they immediately know they must buy. It's old, with a thatched roof, has a garden famed for its narcissi and daffodils, and a prehistoric fort and an ancient yew tree on its land. Most important, it has a beautiful room overlooking church and orchard: 'This will do fine as my study!' Sylvia cries, happy, full of belief in the future. But, as they know before long, they move into a ring of spells and curses, of 'weird luck' and hauntings, a place that, like the innocuous-looking house in a horror movie, will bring them to a bad end. They may even sense it as they push open the door and walk in. For they will sublet the Chalcot Square flat to a couple, David and Assia Wevill, he Canadian and she of Russian-German parentage, with stories of a childhood in Berlin and growing up in Tel Aviv.

The Flat, July 1961

A table is to Ted the magic plank: walk it and the writer pressing on the firm, dark wood

96

drops straight down into the imagination, dizzying, blue, fathoms deep. Or into—as he sees for Sylvia—a catacomb where Otto smiles up, long buried yet still possessor of an eye that's piercing blue.

A table that is the property of Mr and Mrs Hughes has been advertised in the local paper, and just two people come to view it. 'I'll be making another one once we're in Devon,' announces the proprietor of the table when the couple walk in. And Ted runs his hand along the place where his and Sylvia's poems grew and changed and finally slid from the wood into life. 'Try it' He gazes at the man, who is a poet, nervous at meeting the already famous Hughes—and just as he keeps his eyes from the man's wife, the two women gaze at each other and then away.

'We came about the flat,' says the beautiful woman, whom Ted stares at at last, and whose black hair makes him think of a wild horse that gallops over Mongolian plains. Her skin glows with reddish freckles, so she seems a Danae, caught in a shower of gold. 'But we'll take the table too!' And she laughs.

The husband doesn't look at Sylvia, who is not famous yet. A housewife, she moves nervously around the table as if to protect and polish it, rather than as if she has set words, crossed out and rearranged and thrown together again in a gene pool of possibilities, on a pad of paper on the surface of the wood.

In the jumble of explanations that follows—
the two ads placed in different periodicals, the
misunderstanding and the resolution—the
table and the flat begin to symbolize a future
where the two men and the two women will
join their lives.

'We'd love to take the flat—' David, the
quiet husband, less nervous now.

'Don't you want the lovely table to write
on?' A voice surprisingly harsh from Assia, the
voice of a woman accustomed to commanding
servants in the English shires—though this is
learned, tone inflections laid on in Canada and
Tel Aviv.

'I am delighted.' The serious American
voice of Sylvia, considered, grave.

'That's done, then.' Ted, hugely pleased,
wrenches open the fridge door and pulls out a
bottle of white wine. Soon, they will sit around
the table and talk as if they had all been
friends.

'You'll come and see us in Devon?' Sylvia
says, still the hostess, the housewife, as Ted
deflects his gaze from the dazzle of the woman
who will live here when he has gone. And for a
brief moment, as they finalise matters, Sylvia
sees herself reflected in the pale blue eyes of
the beautiful Assia Wevill, herself but other.

*   *   *

At least six months have passed since the

knowledge of coming trouble flashed across Sylvia's mind, and the lightning perception has been followed by a long roll of months of establishing herself as a countrywoman (as she sees it), a walker on land that is theirs (though she means hers).

By the time her son has been born, the winter mud has been succeeded by hedges (too high, constricting) that are blue with violets, and Sylvia has forgotten her sense of foreboding, in that life before the move to the country, in the flat in Chalcot Square.

The Story of Atalanta

The Summer Before the Move

Ted cares for his small daughter, he gives the mornings to Sylvia to work in and has the afternoons for his own writing; and sometimes it's the other way around. The clock ticks; the pink-and-white gingham covers on the cradle stir in a soft summer breeze. London is full of sweet smells. You can hear the sea lions in the zoo in Regent's Park—and on nights when the moon is full the wolves bay, as if a fairy tale really has come to enclose the young, handsome father and the fair mother and the child who doesn't know yet the difference between a beast and a man.

Today, Ted is haggard from a sleepless night with a teething baby. For all the work his wife, so committed to perfection, puts in, he too sweeps and dusts and cooks and cares for the child. All night she was on his knee, and as she clung to him there, he wrote—of another birth, a rebirth and death in the *Tibetan Book of the Dead*, with its cycle of forty-nine days, its showing of a way out of the here-and-now world. As he wrote, both he and the infant were born, and died, and turned one into the other, in the endless repeating pattern—and when Sylvia came in to find them still together in the grey dawn they stayed, talking in low voices, in the room where the words had come against the crying and waking of the child.

If Sylvia dreams of her childhood, she struggles to set down memories that she knows are all that make her live. If she despairs, her husband the poet comforts her. But both poets know they're in a race. And only one of them, in the end, can survive.

Ted thinks of love, and of the race the mythical Atalanta was not allowed to win. He muses, as he sits by the cradle, with its tiny rustlings and moans, on the handicaps his wife must carry with her through her life. For, however punctiliously he keeps to his timetable with the child, however much he loves and however often he comforts his wife, he knows she cannot win.

Ted has thrown the first golden apple—the

baby, innocent in its cot—to the running beauty, the Atalanta/Sylvia he must outstrip and conquer in the race for fame.

And Sylvia has chased after the golden apple, searching in the crevices of sleepless nights, wandering, lost, in milky mists where words haven't even been invented.

Already, she begins to feel the anger that must come when the gods threaten play with blood, lust, and death: she hates the pretty BBC programme editor who takes Ted out to lunch and returns him like a big cat, purring. She watches her hair grow greasy and lank, for there is never time to wash and set, no time at all to make it gold like the happy wife in all the best fairy tales. Sylvia is sharp-tempered, and Ted's friends, those who dislike her, show their animosity in little hints at her extravagance, or her self-centred greedy habits. Poor Sylvia! She senses even now, but only at the worst of times, naturally (at other times she is radiant, and she does love the child), that she simply cannot win. Presentiments of further golden apples thrown her way make her abstracted, she dreams almost nightly of the death of Otto.

That was in the summer Assia Wevill came to 10 Chalcot Square—and took first the flat, then the husband, then everything.

Lolita,1962

Devon submits to early summer, the rivers fill

101

and swell and chestnut candles stand stiff as bottle brushes on trees so thick with leaves there's no chance of indulging in pure thought or reasoning.

Ted sits fishing by the still, brown pool where no one can find or catch him. He's hard to distinguish from the tree that appears to embrace him, with its arms stuck in a coat of scaly bark, as it leans out over the river. Hair short, in a pudding-bowl cut Sylvia derides, and trunk shrouded in mackintosh and baggy cords, he could have been here since before the time the meadows were cut and portioned off, a part of the rigid system of ownership and order he has always disliked. He could be dreaming of the rivers he knows run through wild terrain, in Scotland or on the far coast of Galway, where he might disappear as gently into the sea as an otter or a seal. His crouch, resigned and watchful, over the slow-moving Devon stream, expresses an impatience once again to be free. The cast goes into the deep pool. No salmon here, no flash of pink granite visible between boulders that hold back the rushing water: just the knowledge of a trout, large, brown and camouflaged as he, lurking ten feet down on a bed of mud and pebbles.

Nothing. He reels in, with a sound that sets up a rustling in the foliage behind him; but he's deaf to it, intent now on the capture of the prey he's seen twice here already, rising to his fly and then going down again.

One more cast. The hook and Mayfly go high in the air—and then comes a cry, like the soft call of a bird, followed by a burst of giggles. A face framed in frizzy hair peers down from the tree. Ted looks up, frowning at first. Then he bursts out laughing, at the girl he has caught, by the hem of her dress patterned with lozenge shapes of orange and blue. He knows her, of course he does. Her name is Kate.

When the birds aren't at it, making their own glades of song in the garden at Court Green, the Hughes' new house at North Taunton, a child is crying, comforted by the nonsense sounds her minder has learned from her own mother, who has sent young Kate over from New Zealand to spend a year with relatives in the old country. The farm machinery makes a noise too, as it groans and shudders in crooked lanes made more tortuous by a dazzle of cow parsley in full white bloom. And boys shout on their way to school, the burgeoning season adding inches to their height as they pause to lean over the bridge across the river and scrutinize their futures in the hurrying minnows there. Everything—children, sounds, the sweet pull of the year—draws the poet from his desk and out into the open air, to the side of the pram tucked safely under a tree. He loves his baby son—of course he does—but wasn't that the growl of the bus he heard among the rush of other noises a minute or so ago, in the lane? Isn't it time for the little baby-sitter, at present helping her employer in the kitchen, to run out, satchel struggling to gain a hold on her back, and board the bus to Okehampton High School, to join her cousins there? After lessons, they'll lie in the grass, talk about the school certificate exams they're about to take—then Kate will return to the baby-monotony of Court Green.

Kate Hands is fifteen years old, she wears a brace on her teeth and round rimless glasses that appear to enlarge the rest of her plump, almost unformed face and leave her eyes as small and unconcerned as ever they were. She has a body that is unguessable, even in the green-and-white gingham dress that is the summer uniform at Okehampton High: there's always a grey cardigan, from Monica in Exeter, or a blazer with proud gilt buttons, to obscure it. Her legs, which start from the dress without a hint of promise of a thigh, or even a curve higher up, go down like young trees into white cotton socks. She has a crush on Ted. And he feels the unknown, unfinished quality of Kate Hands in the same way a farmer knows a heifer or a sheep, sniffing the air and walking around the animal on sale for a sense of its coming worth. In all this mayhem of the month of May, this riot of rain and sun and maypole colours in the hedges and on the high green banks, Kate Hands is as refreshing and uncluttered as a blank page.

Yes—here she comes! Mrs Hughes is not as kind to poor Kate as she might be, perhaps— to augment the two-and-six an hour the girl has learned to expect from other houses where she scrubs and peels and soaks, at least a bun or sandwich for her long school day. But the lady is quiet, keeps herself to herself. Or she speaks in a tongue Kate can't understand: only this morning she'd said she could hear the swallows up on the roof. 'They're taking it, straw by straw, to build their nests,' she'd said. She's a bit strange—she looks tense, so Kate thinks, a good deal of the time, and can't wait to get to her desk when the girl arrives to take over the care of the children. She doesn't gab on, like Mrs Carson—or ask embarrassing personal questions, like the vicar's wife.

What Kate feels for Mr Hughes is something completely different. She knows— again, just as the judged animal knows—the interest that is being taken in her; even though, naturally, such things as sex or sexually interested men, in the heart of England in this age still constrained since the end of the war, are quite unknown to her. England is a quiet place, in this time of growing prosperity and tight regulations. There are no rapists in this neck of the woods. The last burglary was ten years ago. Kate, even if some part of her acknowledges the approaching theft of her virginity, is utterly ignorant of the ways of the great world.

It is also known to 'old' Mrs Hands (Kate's great-aunt came from West Dorset, Kate's mother and siblings emigrated to New Zealand) that Kate can't think of anyone except the good-looking man who dresses like a country tramp and walks like a soldier. Mrs Hands wishes Kate wouldn't play her little Dansette gramophone so loudly when the new owner of Court Green passes, and lean out the window, her elbows splayed on the sill like ham bones.

'I've got myself a walking, talking, living doll . . .' Here, although old Aunt Hands is ignorant of the meaning of the Cliff Richard song, it is the draft of the new age as it blows even as far as Devon and seizes girls of fifteen along its way. The Beatles, barely known, are recording their first hit. From the land of Lolita, where the good-looking man of thirty-one has been the past two years, comes the wicked allure of the schoolgirl; and from England come the sounds to bring her suddenly, shudderingly, to life. Kate, unknowingly, is trying to show off a type of female that simply didn't exist when he himself was in his first youth: the nymphet, the teenager, rabid with desire and sticky gum.

Rivals in the Kitchen

There's a lull in the kitchen, in the house where there is never any calm. Beyond the pale walls, streaked with vapour trails from soups long boiled-over and gone, outside the haven the kitchen has now become, crimson stairs march upward, to an Arctic whiteness. The house is tense, braced in the colours he dreads and she insists on: the carcass colours of splitting apart.

No one coming in would guess anything other than a reign of contentment and labour here. Rewards are spelled out in the treasure-chest glow of floor on wall: a dawn that holds the rosiness of children, birth pains and dry nights in the white hours when the words won't come, all quite forgotten now. It's perfect: life and work and love together.

Traces of the disruption to come are—surprisingly, for two people so sensitive to every symbol and portent—ignored. A bee, escaped from a hive as symmetrical and planned as the Devon farmhouse where they find themselves so happy, flies sometimes into the kitchen, large, unseeing as a country policeman, and flies out again. An old woman with groceries in shopping bags comes to the gate and stands looking in at the scene of domestic happiness. That night a barn owl flies against the window, Chinese ghost-face pressed up against the glass. But no one pays any attention to the flutter and heave of bad things to come. Apart from the dreams of her father, and her sudden views of Ted as her father—stooping over a pile of clothes on a chair, the back of his head in the tall chair downstairs with the newspaper raised like a sheet over his eyes—Sylvia thinks, and writes home, only of the wonderful roundedness of their life.

The new people are coming this evening. They are the last link with London: when they return there, it will be to the flat where Ted and his wife and their baby girl lived. David and Assia will be London; and their country hosts will remain here forever, where the first shoots of daffodils show themselves as early as midwinter and long months stretch out before rain falls on the dark leaves. Ted and Sylvia, striding and owning the ground, fill out like ships in sail as the guests are blown toward them. David and Assia will take over the flat, the bills, the bone-ache of the walk from Chalk Farm underground station. The new, strident colours of Court Green fade in the heat of an English summer's day as if to welcome them. And no one notices, or at least refers to, the ominous preparations for the impending disaster. The telephone throws out its cord, across the hall. The scarlet rib cage of steps to the upper landing grows shadows along the length of Wilton pile: a man's falling body sometimes, at other times a crooked elbow caught in the spokes of the stair rail. When it grows dark—so late, out here in the West Country—the old woman rides across the moon, still clutching her paper bags.

Only another hour to go, and the casserole bubbles on the electric cooker (no gas here, in the country, no blue flames licking, inviting, when the father-dreams grow so intense that she must come downstairs and sit in the tall chair, watching the curtains fold like bats' wings across the black night). Potatoes—they're yet to be peeled. But Ted does them—and though she doesn't like to see him skin a rabbit or hare or twist the neck of a chicken with a snap that sends her thumbs tingling, she likes to see him peel potatoes. Eyes are scooped out, brown fuzzy coats stripped adroitly, exposing a white, hard belly. Tonight, Ted is late to come down and empty the potato bucket into the sink. Is he reading a story upstairs, to his little daughter? Or is he—as Sylvia suspects, and she knows even the kitchen suspects, as the clock grins from the wall and the blue-and-white-striped eggcups begin to appear first convivial and then alarmed—is he readying himself for the visit from Assia and David. Of course, he doesn't know them well—he and Sylvia have met them only once when they came to look around the north London flat—but what is the need to

109

wash or change clothes, which isn't Ted's custom anyway? The casserole, chuckling on the hot plate, knows the answer. In the groan of an emptying cistern and the thrum of pipes as the last of the hot water comes grudgingly up into the ancient bath sounds the death rattle of married love.

Sylvia herself has changed for the occasion: as if, like an actress preparing for one last role, she senses the necessity for flawless presentation. Who changes, in the depths of the country, for dinner? Who is this young, smiling woman, blonde as an advertisement model, who stands in a swirl skirt, high heels, a plunging black V-neck top, beside the bucket where the potatoes lie unpeeled? She gazes down at them, and their sooty black eyes return her gaze. A moment of panic disturbs the umpteenth stir of the lamb and carrot casserole, and a fleck of scorching gravy lands on her hand, her writing hand, the hand Ted says will tell her story, if she can only find it one day. But the story is about to come in the door. And when her husband does—the husband of this paragon of domesticity, of all-American virtue and new technology—it is to find his wife crying. Sylvia always makes too much of a fuss. A headache, a tiny burn from the recipe she worries over hour after hour, is enough to bring grief, anger, hysteria. Only Ted, as he stands there so handsome in a freshly ironed (by her) check shirt and corduroy trousers, is caught suddenly by the scene. The myth unfolds before him: betrayed wife, cauldron on a leaping fire, the young son she has thrown in to stew there, ready for her adulterous husband to feast on. Her revenge. But the crime hasn't been committed yet. And Ted goes to empty the potato bucket into the sink, watching as water sluices off the dirt, and grit lodges in the drainer, like a child's mud pie.

*　　*　　*

You know when you see a face that's not like any other. The face of a saint—or a painted woman—a face glimpsed once behind a screen or grille, the intricate pattern cutting out the hollow of the cheek, or giving prominence to a burning eye. A secret, Talmudic, Eastern face, made to be half-hidden, yet brazen when it emerges from the shadow or the smoke. A Russian face, hunted in pogroms, infinitely suffering, resisting yet praying for pain—this is the face Ted sees as the kitchen door opens and the guests appear. How did they come in? But of course, this isn't London, and the newly settled Mr and Mrs Hughes are still taken aback when people simply wander in. Especially when the owner of such a face is one of them. He sees steppes, and wolves in a winter forest where only icicles grow on the tall pines. Assia's beauty, as cold as the Snow

Queen's but with pale blue eyes you could throw a stone into and watch it sink. This is what Ted sees, and as he sees it he changes from boy to man.

So what does Sylvia see, she whose face is red now, from the casserole's heat—and from the tears she's had to wipe away herself with the kitchen towel? Does she see the far side of her own childhood, the young girl her father, Prince Otto, sent on a packed train to the death Sylvia sometimes contemplates for herself? Does she see, in the face of this icon Madonna who walks toward her smiling— smiling just like Sylvia—the gold haze of martyrdom, the washed-blue eyes downcast as if she knows even now a cause for guilt, a knowledge of coming retribution? Is the stranger who has come unannounced right into the heart of the house, the kitchen, already her usurper? For Assia is certainly the 'other', the reverse side of the coin, the dark, forbidden country across the world from America, where Sylvia, in her brightness, fair as day, stands for order, discipline, and unacknowledged cruelty.

Flamboyant, humble Assia. As David talks of the long train ride down to Devon, the winding lanes and claustrophobic green hills, Sylvia looks helplessly on. For the beautiful Russian, who has caused her to feel herself fade and evaporate, to grow pale in the malevolent rays of the dark goddess, the moon, has gone to the sink with Ted and is picking out the potatoes. He's laughing—and protesting—she insists. And he hands her a sharp little knife. Sylvia knows the knife the way she knows a friend or a child. It goes into Assia's hand, which is covered with rings: tourmaline, topaz, turquoise, silver from the tribes of Southeast Asia beaten to the shape of a lion's head. And with the knife she digs out the potatoes' little squinting eyes.

*   *   *

The oracle doesn't speak; the forest where she lives provides the answers, in the blue light over the carpet of pine needles, in the rushing sound of the river as it sweeps down the side of the mountain, in the scissor squawk of the jay. You can see the oracle by the flames she has around her: sunset silk from the Ganges, gold bangles and coins that dance at her wrists. The oracle is silent, looks into the eyes of her prey. Her lashes are barbed wire, knotted black and frozen with tears. Her teeth are hammered from iron. She'll eat her rival alive.

Why can't anyone see what's going on? Why do the powerful mask their identities so effortlessly? Surely it's plain this woman has chosen to be tongueless, mistress of the Mysteries, for the sole purpose of trapping the prize trophy. She'll keep him underground for the duration, his children will falter then grow away from him, the crops will wither and no fresh season will come. But she won't mind, and neither will he. She'll act out the initiation again and again, the secret of the origin of life. And she mustn't speak—her cut-glass accent would ruin everything.

Sylvia brings the casserole to the table and lifts the lid. In the steam that rises she sees the Gypsy fortune-teller across the table, her stolen child exchanged for a robber prince. The yew tree in the churchyard beyond the window sheds its fur and stands bare, decked with glass baubles. And the house pulls in its stays, puckers its lips in the presence of a witch.

Ted escapes to childhood, to long days that end in half-light, the fall of dying deer and hare as he walks and shoots, tramping miles over ling and fell. He sees the woman who woos his wife, as they linger at table—and what he sees is a huntress, as skilled and ruthless as himself. Then, when he looks again at her, he sees a victim awaiting the order to kill—and behind her in the blue air of the death camp, a line of old women, high-kicking their legs, dancing in a forced mimicry of youth.

Whose is the death warrant here? Sylvia gazes at Assia and speaks in the low, earnest voice that covers her terror of insanity. Assia gazes back at her. Images come before him, of the hanged man on a tarot card, by the bread bin against the wall; of a long, pointed-snout fish swimming upstream against a torrent. There is a commotion at the door: a child, woken by the dreams the strange woman has brought, runs in. And the visitor, ambushed, surprised, cries out a greeting in her impossible voice. The spell is broken.

* * *

Neither husband nor wife can sleep, in this house no one can recognise. The moon comes in on the crimson stairs and makes a river of blood, an artery that runs from top to bottom of a building grown white and precarious. The wind drops, and the guests can be heard twisting and turning in their beds. Pictures dance before eyes: Assia, with the great golden fish her dream has caught, struggles and sweats on this hot summer night. Her husband lies beside her, pretending to sleep. In the room where Sylvia sits upright, propped against a bolster, a cold, dry breeze presages the arrival of Otto from his tomb. And Ted, the anvil where the new alliance is already forged, lies as still and immovable as stone.

Each hour of the night, marked by the church tower clock, marks a calendar of coming fatalities. The minute hand creeps like a blade across the frozen hours as births and deaths and murders are rung out. The house beyond the churchyard shows a light, suddenly, in an upper window. Sylvia can't stand it anymore. She'll read—archaeology and anthropology, news of men buried in ice, books on ants and apes, anything. But still she'll see the morning as it dons its black cap and calls her down to the kitchen. Sunday lunch, more potatoes—already, as they go into boiling water, she hears their angry hiss.

This morning, when it comes, is hotter than the night before, and a haze that's like honey spilled in a saucer attracts flies and insects into the house. The kitchen window is open, and bees—not the kind Sylvia rules over, in their city down in the field, but small bees that like the honeysuckle and lavender in the garden at Court Green—make a soft buzzing outside. Sylvia can't bear it: she goes to shut the window, bang! And the baby crawling across the floor sends up a scream.

Ted sits so still that he could be away, leaving behind him a memory of himself that sits at the table in the check shirt of the night before. Nothing happened, I'm still here, the figure seems to proclaim: the night is cancelled, the witch never came. But in his still face are the lineaments of satisfaction; and Sylvia sees them, though she cannot guess the truth. For her husband, the man she writes home about with such verve and devotion, came down to the kitchen so early that there was no one about, and he sat at this very chair at the table. He looked at the washing-up the two women had done together—and that he and the stranger's husband had dried together, as if offering a bonded reassurance to the wives, as if to say that husbands are all that matter and who gets which is unimportant—he looked across at the empty casserole, mystery drained and undignified, upside down by the sink—and as he did so, the room disappeared, hidden from him by a wall of white cloth.

Inside the nightdress that now enveloped him, Ted felt the heat of Assia's body and smelled her night-smells. He stood shivering beside rivers and plunged his head between her breasts.

Then, lifting her great white net high in the air, Ted's captor walked away from him across the kitchen, as Sylvia and her baby came in.

When Sylvia hears Assia's dream—of the golden fish and half-formed child that throbs within its eye—she knows she's done for, the battle's lost. And it's later than she thought, the day is wearing on. She throws potatoes into the cast-iron pot full of cold water. They'll peel them when they're cooked—it would never do to serve them in their skins.

*   *   *

The next day Ted leaves for London. 'I must see you in London'—the words spoken in the hush of the kitchen, when Sylvia was last seen making her way down the lane—or so the lovers (for she knows they're in wish, in longing, in fantasy, the most perfect of lovers) must have thought. But turning at the end of the path, stooping to check the bursting buds on the lilies and the old roses, Sylvia went unobserved as she dodged back, under cover of trees, to the house. She's accustomed to this way of spying on the husband she now mistrusts, and she hears herself discussed, in her own fantasies, as suffering from paranoid jealousy. Well then, she is! She's jealous and she has every right to be, for 'I must see you in London' translates, just as she expected, into a nervy and jumpy declaration, after the weekend guests have left, of a pressing need to take the Exeter train to the city in the morning. Work: Money: a matter of urgency.

All day after he's gone, the garden is filled with the activities of the busy, happy woman Sylvia describes herself as being, in letters to her mother. That Aurelia is due over from America soon makes the mask all the more essential. She must never know of this betrayal and its enormity; nor of the unhappiness that seeps into the passages of the old house like a ghostly rain. She must see the ideal couple Sylvia represents: busy, yes; happy, yes; but above all, successful. The children show no sign of being affected by the miasma Sylvia feels she is responsible for creating (for, as Ted denies everything except the constant presence of Otto as an exacerbating factor in Sylvia's 'states', she must bear the brunt of the blame). The children are healthy and happy and well, even if their mother cries and goes to her worktable earlier and earlier each day, in the dawn finding words that come at first with difficulty, so covered with the dew of night-forgetting are they. And Aurelia must see the garden grow as blooming and beautiful as the children. All day long, on the day Ted takes the nine a.m. express to London, Sylvia cuts weeds and builds a willow bower to train the roses over, and pulls wisteria along the crumbling old walls of the house.

When night finally comes, late in the month before midsummer in the West Country, so late that her back is aching and she has lost track of the time, Sylvia comes indoors from the dusk garden. The children were put to bed hours ago. She's tired; she'd be content after all the labour if it weren't for the dread of sleep that grips her.The dreams: the atrocities: misshapen, tortured men and women; camps with their implacable guards; gouged-out eyes, corpses everywhere. And Ted won't be here to help her out of the nightmares when they come, he'll be in London with the woman he has fallen for. Fallen—Sylvia sees his dizzy descent, down the steep spiral of the Tower of Love—fallen, there's no other word for the abject state she saw him in this morning when, abruptly, he walked out of the kitchen and down the hall to the long journey away from her. She knows the fall is fatal, this time; but her dread of discovery later, of the horrors that will be revealed to her in sleep, is compounded by the strange feeling that she has fallen too. 'You're fascinated by her,' Ted said, triumphant, after Assia and her husband left in the waiting taxi and drove off as if nothing unusual had taken place, as if they were just normal weekend guests. 'Fascinated!'

And so, as Sylvia reflects, suddenly too tired to stay one minute longer in the lonely kitchen, with only the bundles of dried thyme and rosemary so neatly housewife-tied as company —so she is. She has a sense of a bond, a join between herself and the stranger with her kohl-rimmed eyes who has left herself indelibly here, even after so short a visit. Sylvia sees Assia as a bonfire in orange silk, consuming her home, her husband, her happiness. But she knows, as the flames crackle and burn on the upper landing, that nothing will prevent her from rising as early as ever, and sitting down to write before the children wake.

The night contains none of the agonies of the Holocaust Sylvia expects and prays to be delivered from. There is no Otto Plath, rising from the Prussian town in the Polish Corridor where he was born, setting off on a fiery charger to murder and exterminate the Jews. There are no death camps. The beautiful stranger who has taken Ted doesn't lie emaciated at the feet of Sylvia's father. The

120

obvious nightmares are absent—but, as she lies tossing on the bed she knows will never again contain a moment of rest, of married joy, a woman comes in her dreams to Sylvia. She is Procne, wife of Tereus, king of Thrace. Her story—and her warning—is this.

'You were fated to marry, and now that you know yourself to be no longer yourself, you are fated for the time that remains to you to seek out the other—for it is only when you find and come to terms with her that you will find yourself again.

'This is easier said than done. Even if it means the committing of an act of desperation, of self-immolation or the harming of another, you cannot live beside yourself as marriage has taught you to do. You must return to inhabit your being. And the woman you seek, however near or far from her you may think yourself to be, must be as willing as you to act in unison with you—as close, as affectionate and loyal, as a sister.'

*   *   *

Sylvia, half-awake, sits slowly up in bed, her eyes on the woman who is no more substantial than the moonlight that comes into the room, a white column of light that neither approaches nor recedes. She feels the paralysis of fear, she feels her jaw drop as her body slackens, she feels the black weight of sleep.

Procne tells of her marriage to the king, and as she talks of the mountains where she and Tereus rode seven days and seven nights to reach the kingdom of Thrace, the sleeping figure in the bed in the white room at the head of the stairs that are the colour of dried blood in the night light half-wakes again to hear the tale she already knows so well.

*   *   *

The new palace, with its floors of garlanded marble, and banqueting tables where strangers, entertained in magnificence by the great king, devoured birds within birds and whole boars that turned night and day on a spit above a fire piled with golden pinecones, brought only sadness to Tereus's queen.

She had lost her sister, Philomela. She dreamed of her in the gardens where the splendour of long hedges and clipped peacocks and exotic trees served only to increase her terrible loneliness.

Without Philomela, Procne was only half herself. They had never been apart—though often, when they were together, they felt no love for each other, merely that their mother had borne them one after the other, twins and yet separate. Each one knew the other, so they thought, better than herself.

Until one day this sense of knowing and not-knowing, trust and fear of betrayal, was tested to the utmost.

Procne begged her husband to go to her own country and bring her sister back to her. In those days, at the time of this story, the daughter of a powerful man could refuse to leave her land when giving her hand in marriage. Think of Penelope, who, all the years Odysseus roamed the world and fell into the hands of vicious women, mourned the fact that she had left her island, her father's and hers, to marry the man who abandoned her for so long.

*   *   *

Sylvia in her half-waking dream walks down the alleys where long hedges form a geometry of desire. In the shadows she stands and gazes up at a Thracian moon. The jasmine scent of Assia, distilled with night-wetness from the folded hills beyond the window of the old house, draws her to leave the bed and stand, while the column of light, the robed woman who has come to visit her, spells out the remainder of her tale.

*   *   *

'Tereus   agreed   with   my   demand,   he

understood my isolation in the country that had been known to him—each rock, each mossy bank and leaping stag—since he was a child. He said goodbye to our son, Itylus, and he assured me he would bring my sister, Philomela, back to me.

'But what happened was entirely different. When Tereus did return from the long journey, he returned alone. He spoke of the death of Philomela. And while I wept, I wondered that I had felt nothing, for if my sister suffered, I did, and the other way around.

'So I felt little surprise when the tapestry came, brought running by a faithful servant who had witnessed the atrocities of Tereus.'

*　　　*　　　*

Sylvia stands by the window of the room that is white in the moonlight. She hears her children breathe and turn in their cots, in the little rooms where the shade from the yew tree brings peace and darkness. She tenses herself for the last words.

*　　　*　　　*

'The tapestry showed the barbaric cruelty of Tereus. I saw the beauty of my sister, even in the crude pictures her poor needle sketched for me there. It was an elfin beauty, such as you see in woods, such as you read about in books. I saw Tereus rape her, and cut out her tongue.

'My sister was dumb. The tongue came to me in the palace gardens like a snake, speaking of the love between Philomela and my husband, the king.

'I knew it was false. Tereus had raped Philomela. But what, said the tongue as it lay before me on a moonlit night such as this one—what if Philomela fell in love with Tereus after she had been raped?

'I killed the snake with the pitchfork the gardeners keep leaning against the wall of the temple where it is always cold and dark. And I wept again, that thoughts and suppositions such as these could come to me.'

*   *   *

A child's cry breaks Sylvia's dream: as she hurries to the landing outside her room, she feels the white clothes her night visitor wears, as they brush against her in the fading light of the moon.

She hears the scream of Itylus, the son of Tereus and Procne, as his mother and her sister, Philomela, plunge him into the depths of the great cauldron over the fire.

And she wakes, finally, as Tereus, unknowing, is served and eats the bleeding gobbets of his own loved son. The feast glitters and disappears. The moon wanes. She hears the great cry of horror, the primeval shout that carries all the way across the world and wakes Ted and Assia as they copulate under a smoky sky.

Nothing has come to disturb the quiet of the house in Devon as Sylvia slept and dreamed— of twins, of sisters, of another who is also herself.

*　　　*　　　*

In the long week that has passed since her dream (Sylvia knows the myth's ending: Philomela, running, then flying away from her fate, became a nightingale; Procne a swallow who haunts the houses where children live with their parents; and Tereus a hoopoe)—in the days that flatten out toward the summer solstice and the arrival of Aurelia from America, Ted returns home and goes on as if nothing had changed.

But as the week grows taut with the tension between Sylvia and Ted, the destruction of their lives together is spelled out, as chance would have it, in just the way chosen by Procne's sister in the era before the marking of the passage of time.

The postman comes. Sylvia, who likes to sit by the window of her study looking out, gazes from her table as the little red van stops in the lane and the burly man in dark blue with a red stripe (the uniform, like the scarlet of the van, is exciting to her: there may be poems accepted by *The New Yorker*, or a letter from her mother, saying how much she longs to see them all) comes to the door and bangs the knocker. The baby is woken in his pram and gives a long, interrogative cry. Ted is nowhere to be seen. So Sylvia, torn from her ninth draft of a poem, less pleased now that she must be the one to answer the door, goes down the stairs and lets him in. It must be a parcel: one that won't fit in the letter box that admits the fan mail for Ted, the invitations to read, dramatise, translate. It's a gift for him, probably: already, Sylvia feels the rush of jealousy, a high pain in her chest, blurred vision as she peers at the wildly written label on the battered wrapping paper.

The parcel is for her. She signs for it, absentmindedly: Mrs S. Hughes, as the directions make her out to be. She feels bored, irritated—if the package isn't addressed to Sylvia Plath it can't be books or anything interesting. She frowns as she pinches the corners and carries it in. Someone has knitted her a sweater, perhaps—but the thought is preposterous. Not for the first time, Sylvia thinks how much she hates most of Ted's friends, and how unlikely they are to knit a garment for her. Remembering this has already spoiled her morning. The poem sits like an undigested meal stuck high up in the gullet of the house.

The parcel contains a square of tapestry. Needlepoint, as Sylvia sees, casting her mind back to a conversation—false, fulsome as she had thought at that time, on Assia's part— about needlework and her love for it: Sylvia had remained quite cool. A square of empty white canvas with, at the centre, a red rose. A note, from Assia, declaring that since their conversation she found herself unable to resist the giving of the uncompleted tapestry to Sylvia. Sylvia might like to go on with it: it should be enough to cover a chair.

The dream returns, as the square of canvas with its little holes is turned in the sunlight in the hall, from side to side. The red rose gleams like a fresh wound in its hard white border.

When Ted comes back from his walk to the farm for milk, he sees his wife, again through a window but downstairs, in the kitchen, where all the acts of the drama were first played out. He sees her hold the needlepoint square up toward him, as he stands outside the window in the dry June grass. He steps back—then, as if he's seen nothing at all to surprise him, he lifts the latch and walks in.

The scarlet bloom never does get its accompaniment of dark green leaves. With Aurelia coming, there is so much to do. And then, Sylvia is never entirely sure what this message from the woman who has taken Ted's heart and soul from her is supposed to signify.

That she's a sister of the wronged wife, under the skin? That she's also a victim of the monstrous tyrant, and unable to escape his rapacious will?

Or is the red rose, with its creeping petals of blood, a message from a vampire, a woman who will drive her rival into the whiteness she identifies as death?

In the next weeks, as her mother watches in horror, Sylvia wrenches the telephone cord from the wall when Assia calls and in bass tones asks for Ted. There's the chance of an escape, sometimes, to visit a friend in a neighbouring village—Elizabeth Compton, the only woman who really seems to love Sylvia. But rage reigns supreme: Sylvia makes a bonfire of her husband's manuscripts and her own letters and she dances around it, feeding the flames with his hair clippings, nails, anything. She has become a witch; silent and demure, the other woman awaits Ted's more and more frequent visits to North London. The sister whose tongue has been cut out may suffer, but for now she is the victor, the new wife.

On the day Sylvia drives the station-wagon off the road in Devon and onto an airfield, her mother begins to know true despair. Instead of crawling downward, as her daughter had done in Wellesley all those years ago, she seems obsessed with clouds, and heights. When they come to lead her from the scene of the near-accident, Sylvia is staring up into the blue. A tiny plane, with just enough room for a pilot and a passenger, is dancing like a daddy-long-legs along the turf runway. Then, as if thrown up by a passing gust of wind, it takes off and is soon invisible in the summer sky.

Cats

Assia Wevill is wearing a new kind of boot, black leather and thigh-high, and a daffodil-yellow box jacket and short skirt. She walks the length of the lion house as if unseeing of the animals prowling or sleeping behind bars. Assia is an exotic animal herself, so the stretch of leather, stocky frame, and glinting eyes announce: there's no need for Ted to pause by the caged cats when there's something like Assia on hand.

Assia works for an advertising company that handles the Tory party's account. She's known for her witty one-liners and her daring. Anyone who labels her 'insecure' is only paying her the highest imaginable compliment. Because women who haven't had the spark crushed out of them, women who are as ready as Assia to play any practical joke, risk offending the boss, take on the wildest wager, find, if they don't wish to be labelled a Jezebel or worse, that 'insecurity' is the most acceptable excuse for immoral behaviour. When the Tory party comes a cropper in a year's time with Christine Keeler and the Profumo affair, the agency will need plenty of recruits with both the verve and insecurity of Assia Wevill. But by then, what Assia will need above all are courage and the ability to stand up to her critics and assailants, in the matter of the death of Sylvia.

Ted walks close to his lover, his eyes feasting on the beasts he visits often. He'll go on to see the leopards and pumas. Assia hasn't noticed yet that he really is more interested in the big cats than in her: he feels their thoughts, and has an understanding with them that he'll never find with any woman. At present, this isn't so evident. Several visitors to the zoo— August tourists, Japanese and American—stop in their tracks when they see Assia, her controlled sexual fury, her leather-clad stride. She knows they're impressed, and can't help herself from shooting a triumphant sideward glance at the poet she won for a bet after telling a workmate a few months back that she was going down to Devon to stay with Ted Hughes and a tenner said she'd come back having hooked him.

Ted, however, fails to catch her eye and stares moodily at a magnificent lion as it pulls at a lump of bleeding flesh. He waits for the thrill of the animal to reach him: the fierceness of the appetite, the terrible distance it has covered already today, pacing unconquered miles of jungle in its tiny cage. The powerful lion smell envelops him and he stands minutes longer, waiting for the magic moment of transmogrification, when Ted becomes the lion and the jungle opens up to him. Assia, who is pretending to be absorbed in a mangy lion with a moulting mane at the far end of the house of exhibits, pouts, then shakes her head slowly so that her own mane, sleek, swings alluringly for the tourists' cameras. Why can't Ted hurry up? There'll be another long visit when the big cats are done—to the aquarium. Assia rather regrets having made up the dream in which a golden pike swims toward her, a foetus throbbing in its eye. Ted will point out pike. The only house Assia likes visiting is the night mammals' house, where bush babies and lemurs, sleeping in the day with such luxury and abandon, make Assia think of where she would really much prefer to be: back in the flat, in bed with Ted.

As Assia thinks of the domesticity that awaits them on this unpleasantly sultry day— she'll talk about having children again, Ted will change the subject or go off into the kitchen, looking for a drink—he is as far from being transported to the Mountains of the Moon by 'his' lion as Assia is (though of course she has no desire to be) by hers. The pictures that rise before his eyes are also domestic, but unlike Assia's vague picture of a

132

small stately home (in appearance similar to a mock-Georgian house in an ad), Ted sees his own home, back in Devon. Over the green hills a fine white fog lifts, and a bright sun shines brightly on the flowers and shrubs he and Sylvia planted together. What happened? Why, of all places, is he in a zoo with someone who has no love for animals, when he could be at home?

The answer is hard to find. Only the restless cat, which has finished feeding now and, seeing its visitor for the first time, begins to pace quickly—then more and more quickly, then, finally, in a walk that is never quite a run but that could outstrip any man, loses itself in the endless, meaningless motion—only the lion seems to shed light on the matter. Assia is forgotten, as he sees his wife behind the bars of her own nature, her madness, her need both to survive and to disappear. His wife is caged, her only freedom a further lunge downward to obscurity. He sees a desperate act—and leans forward across the rail, as if to enter the lion's mouth. As he does so, a hand touches his shoulder, an arm goes around him—which he at first resists. But who can resist Assia? No one, apparently, ever has.

When they go back to the flat, Assia tries to extract a promise, a promise for the future, a pledge to leave home and start up properly with her. As she speaks, she paces the tiny North London sitting room. She needs security—anyone can see that. But it's a quality that adds the finishing touch to Assia's appeal—her obvious insecurity shows her to be human, vulnerable. She has said many times how dissatisfied she is with her life. Truly, she's a poet. And he knows her to be gifted, as well as neurotic and insecure. But right now, as the beautiful Assia walks faster and faster by the barred windows of the high-up room in Tufnell Park, all Ted can see is a great cat, untameable, hungry for his flesh.

Retaliate in Advance

Anyone who believes that an abandoned wife must play her role sweetly and discreetly, even in this age of progress, and even if the abandoned wife is from, as she describes it, 'the land of milk and honey and spin dryers' and might be expected to pack a punch no erring husband will be likely to forget—anyone who believes this is in for a surprise, when it comes to Sylvia.

The summer of 1962 is one of comings and goings, promises and broken promises, lies and good intentions that turn to ash like the letters and books thrown on the bonfire at Court Green.

Sylvia is all energy and force—though, as she loses pounds and dark circles appear beneath her eyes, it would be hard to say where this last leap of force comes from.

She has been injured. With two golden apples—her children, whom she loves—to hold, how can she now win the race?

But first, if the man who swore to be with her forever must now come and go like a little wooden weatherman as he pops in and out of his house—rain for his times with Sylvia, all is crying and recriminations and blunt anger; sun for his idyllic times with Assia, as he guides her to poetry and a true understanding of her inner self—then there will be retaliation. It should have come earlier. But the country is difficult, for the finding of someone new. And there are reconciliations and new starts. Vows to live to Ireland, and then a broken holiday there, where Ted leaves right in the middle, crazy as he tells Sylvia she has always been. (By now he's subject to visions and visitations, faces in portraits that move and speak and advise him to leave his wife immediately.

No one can stand it. Who asks whom to go? Sylvia sees the sea, the spiky female sea urchin on the ocean bed, a white pebble smooth and plain as responsibility anchoring her down. Ted packs, and leaves for London after a long week in August, miserable and bitter. Yeats hadn't saved them in Ireland, though they'd been to his house in Ballylee and shook a crop of real apples, a hundredweight of the bright, red fruit, into sacks and carried them off to the friend's cottage where they were staying. Yeats may save them in London, where, on Fitzroy

Road in Hampstead, with the blue plaque of the poet above the door, Ted and Sylvia must pose as a respectable, contented married couple in order to beat old Professor Trevor Thomas and secure the lease of the upper two floors. (Once the old man moves into the smaller flat, downstairs, there's a feeling of his rancour creeping about the place. It depresses Sylvia; just as the pose she and her lawfully wedded husband had to assume has depressed her, reminded her of the near impossibility of retaliation.) For a single woman with children would not have been taken seriously by the landlords. Money—Sylvia's money, which she accuses Ted of spending on his scarlet woman—money, in this enlightened age, the province and privilege of men—money dominates her life and, now that she has decided on divorce, fills her thoughts day and night. Except for the blue hour, the time before dawn when the poems are written, corrected, rewritten, and set down in concrete, buried in perfection, stiff and cold.

One of the best poems, written when she was still in Devon, foresees the strangling of the will, the absolute powerlessness of the position of this powerful, smiling woman. 'The Rabbit Catcher'—it is her at-length-decided-on title of the poem that tells of killing, his need and love for killing, and her own death, deep in the snare, to come. Ted comes to visit the children, and sets his fingers around a mug—and she sees the little deaths, the sweetness of the deaths as they await him—and she decides it's not too late after all. She'll find someone, and she'll find love. The husband who is free to let himself into her private lair, to see his family when he pleases, won't find her so defeated from now on. Her little death will not await him.

The party is a literary party and Sylvia has been invited in her own right (for once) by her publisher. The Garrick is where it's held: the Eliots are there, and the Spenders; and not Ted, who has forgotten perhaps, or is with Assia, detained by the lies and inventions this most inspired of copywriters thinks up when it comes to preventing him from seeing his wife or friends.

The portraits on the walls of the Garrick amuse and please Sylvia. How glad she is to be away from the country! As she mounts the curving staircase and pulls at her hair in the mirrors of the ladies', she glimpses herself in the incarnation that's now past: rustic housewife, Devon beekeeper with her helmet and veil, mother and daffodil-picker and general dogsbody, while her famous husband enjoyed plaudits from the most distinguished in the land. Now it's her turn! Sylvia will have a salon, entertain writers she admires and encourages—particularly men.

*   *   *

Of course Ted notices within a week or so the change in Sylvia on many of the occasions he calls round to the flat. He knows she's maddened by the lack of privacy their arrangement permits her; and at first he thinks she's inventing a new sense of confidence.

But soon he must admit he sees a new look on the face of his wife. He sees the satisfaction of retaliation—but he sees also, under this mask she tries on, an absolute despair, a frantic need for him. It's as if the man she's seeing—and she must be, in Ted's mind, for there's no other explanation for her different, self-assertive mood—is driving her inexorably toward him. 'When she wasn't seeing me, she was seeing someone else,' he wrote years later to a friend. And the paradox was, though neither could really see it, that the suspicion of another man in the life of the woman he still loved did not make him want her. The opposite took place. The man, who never existed for Sylvia, had split the couple conclusively. This became clear around Christmastime, when Sylvia's unhappiness led her to seek the help of friends and depend on doctors. And then the winter came, with Assia glowing in the heart of it like a red-shaded bedroom lamp you just can't turn off.

THREE

The Chill

Red

Snow in Hampstead drifts down from the Heath and mounts the pavement, to lie there yellowing like a tramp's overcoat, shot through with dogs' piss-holes.

Sylvia's car won't start. Nor will the pipes in the flat carry water. Everything is frozen, except the blue voice in her mind—the voice that frightens off the birds, the winter voice that sings against the cosy promise of a valentine. After all, tomorrow is the day promised for the birds' first coupling: Sylvia knows this, as she knows so much else, from books and poems. Someone from America has sent a red heart on a card. The British don't have love festivals and Mother's Day, not yet. The British, like Sylvia, just have the cold.

There's something about this part of London, this street, this flat on Fitzroy Road, that invites the writing that oozes up through snow from the land of the dead. Is it the ghost of Yeats, who lived here in the house Ted and Sylvia chose together, which brings the perfected landscape of her new poems, the landscape before the edge? Are the spirits Yeats saw and believed in, summoned across London's snowy hills by the coal-eyed medium

141

Madame Blavatsky, now possessing Sylvia? Sometimes, as she pours glasses of milk for her children—and at these times she does see the comforts of the land she's lost: the warmth; the tall fridge in her mother's kitchen; ice tamed in cubes, not growing up against the window pane, strangling the plumbing, forming a murderous rim around the pond high on the Heath—sometimes, as she gazes down into the chalky liquid, Sylvia sees the auras of the women who were here before her. The violet and blue of a woman loved by the poet; a cloud, as grey as the view from the grimy windows is white, that is a woman's dress as she bustles up the stairs. But mostly Sylvia is lonely. The freezing streets lock arms against her. Pollarded trees stand like witches' broomsticks before a sky that holds little but the promise of more snow. And people are as in-turned as the black-windowed houses. No one seems to want to see the American woman, with her white, haunted face and hair that's taken on a metallic hue, in this light, from lack of washing. This is the season of the last brown needle of the thrown-out Christmas tree. The daffodil shoots Sylvia digs for in the hard patch of grass outside the house—in order to remember, to see herself once more with Ted, happy in a picture postcard of yellow tossing blooms—meet her numb, swollen fingers with their own: barely above earth, stubborn, lifeless, hard.

Ted does come, as often as three times a week, to Fitzroy Road, and when he has gone Sylvia writes to a friend that his visits lead her to sigh for lost Edens. Yet today, as she stands—and is so often seen standing by Professor Thomas—at the sitting-room window—and watches him leave, it is more painful than ever. For Ted, arriving with a bashful air, had produced from his pocket a battered sunhat—Yes! her own, bought in Devon in what seems another age—grimy from months in the boot of the car, but still, so it seems to her, holding the sun and happiness she had once known. 'I found this . . .' He stood over her, and she knew he might stay, never return to the woman Sylvia refers to only as 'she'. But the moment passes, as they invariably do. 'Hatty,' Ted says, and the memory of the childish, sentimental word is more painful still. Then the children run in.

For all that, Sylvia will have a party. The car will be made to run. The cocktail outfit in the bedroom of her neat flat has been pulled out, at last. From the little make-up case will come all she needs for the 'very important appointment' she has told her friends the Beckers she must keep this Friday evening: rollers to wind in tresses as fair as they have ever been; lipstick so red in the polar glow it forms a mouth in a page torn from a women's magazine—How to Catch Him! How to Keep Him! How to Tell If He Loves You or Not!

Packed in too is mascara that's tear-proof, as all the best ones are. The dress in its overnight bag stirs as the engine finally begins to thrum and throb. Then it slumps, as Sylvia turns off the ignition key and slams out. Why can't she make up her mind? What is this 'important appointment' for which she must dress so elaborately, anyway?

Of course, it's a question of the children. How can these orphans live if their mother goes out dancing? What would her own mother say, who sent her away to Grammy Schober if anything unusual was taking place? Unusual—abnormal—unnatural—obscene—if Sylvia's mother only knew now how her daughter's life has gone awry! If she could read between the lines! But Sylvia knows how to cover up the spaces between the lines so that her mother will never decipher them. She must be perfect. The children must be clean and sparkling, clever and wise. Everyone knows Sylvia is a perfect mother.

But the baby's milk has dried up. In the sea of whiteness all around there's not a drop to drink. Sylvia's breasts rattle like gourds in her dreams. Then she wakes, to the shrill command of the baby, and goes to the kitchen. Two glasses, where until recently there had been only one needed for the elder of those poor children in their cots. How can she leave them? Surely she must keep her 'important appointment' here?

There's always an obstacle, and Sylvia will use the grumpy old man downstairs as an excuse if friends beg her to entertain, enjoy herself. As if she could! With Professor Trevor Thomas lurking about, putting his dislike out into the hall like a skunk letting off its smell. Hadn't Thomas wanted the flat the young husband and wife paid quickly and in cash to secure? What must he think now, with the husband gone and the wife flooding the place with her frozen pipes and blocked bath? Doesn't he feel it's his right to take those rooms, so that he can put his own grown-up sons into them? He'll lead the little children into the forest while their mother's smiling and talking with a stranger, and he'll leave them there, quite lost.

*   *   *

This time, as Sylvia's friends Jillian and Gerry Becker can see, is going to be different.

The cocktail outfit and make-up case go back into the car. Sylvia has been at the Beckers' for two nights, ranting and sleeping and eating—and sleeping, only to wake and rant again. The children have the Beckers' child near them and the care of Jillian Becker. There is nothing whatever to stop their mother from going to her 'important appointment'. The Beckers are relieved when they wave her goodbye from their step in Islington, not more than a few miles from 23 Fitzroy Road. But they wonder, if not aloud to each other, why the cocktail dress goes with Sylvia wherever she goes, like a costume lugged from place to place by an actress in amateur theatricals? Why did she bring the cosmetics case along, with its suggestion of an evening of 'fun' rather than 'an important appointment'? If the Beckers secretly expect that the appointment is with Ted and is important indeed, so important that every prop is needed to convince him he must return to her, then they say nothing to give away their suspicions.

Sylvia drives carefully past the house with the blue plaque honouring W.B. Yeats and waits until a couple of women, bundled in wool against the cold, have gone right to the end of the road, leaving it empty. She parks the car by the shelf of frozen snow, brown as an old man's tea-stained moustache, that refuses to melt on the pavement outside where she lives. The engine makes a loud roar, and the curtain in the lower floor twitches, as it always does when she drives up. Professor Trevor Thomas is there—of course he is—but this time Sylvia doesn't feel the rage she normally feels at the spying, followed by the inevitable shuffle into the hall. She has better things to do. The make-up case, once laid on the bed upstairs, opens sluggishly, for cold and condensation have jammed the locks. The dress comes finally from the overnight bag that has travelled with her to the Beckers' house and back again. The metallic blue-black top glints in the light from the overhead lamp, and—drawn to the strip of scarlet corduroy that lies on a chair, the stuff half-sewn into curtains for this white room where she sleeps alone—Sylvia throws it around her shoulders and twirls before the mirror.

*   *   *

It's when everything seems too perfect—when, for once, the 'important appointment' can take place, that Sylvia, as so often before, feels the need for change. She'll pull the plan apart and rearrange it on the page: she'll build a new poem. As in art, so in life: it's the desperate desire for sex that drives her to grab the cocktail dress and laugh as she holds it up against her body—still so slim and young! It's sex she must have, sex like the night on Rugby Street, Holocaust Night. Sex that will burn away the freezing black breath of the winter she's lived in since Ted, following like a child as the Pied Piper steps always ahead, went after Assia in her coat of many colours.

She must go now—quickly—as she can feel him preparing to come to her. 'I was there on Saturday in Fitzroy Road for a short time,' he will say later. 'She explained she was going away for the weekend and had to lock up.' Sylvia can hear the excuses and in his coming

147

she can feel his last going, the final decision, the judgment, the execution of her happiness for the rest of time. She throws the improvised scarf of corduroy from her shoulders and it runs in a red gush across the floor. The bare white room grins at her from the mirror—which in turn, as it gazes into a future of non-being, grows blurred, then sheeted. Sylvia's death is in this room, on this hill in the city where the snow on high ground lies undisturbed. She must flee from it, away from the whiteness into red.

But it's too late. He knows, as she does, when she most wants him and when she most needs to escape. The steps are on the stairs, the muffled bang of the closing front door follows him as he comes to her.

'We'll be together again in the summer,' he says. 'We'll be at Court Green together—wait until then!'

And as the months, unimaginable months of a winter that cannot end, unfurl before Sylvia's eyes, she falls back from him and wanders, almost blinded, to the window. Here, she would watch out for him with such hope and longing: here, like a buffoon, he stands behind her, his hands reaching out as if attempting to measure time. Can't he see his offer is an insult, that no woman can be given the date of a resumption of her married life? And as she turns slowly to confront him with the blankness in her face, the months begin to count out in the way she has learned to understand. The months of Assia's pregnancy —indifferent to winter, summer, spring. And when Ted leaves, she knows herself to be more alone than she has ever been.

The car runs smoothly at the start of the journey down from Hampstead into hell. It's Sunday, her children are with friends; Sylvia is at the wheel (this time Trevor Thomas is outwitted and hears no sound of engine, no ice cracking in a puddle as she pulls away). She is out to do business tonight. She's dressed to the nines in a cocktail dress that shows her as the opposite of respectable, provincial, child-smothered, when she arrives in Soho. What will be described, just three days later, as 'Ted's current address in Soho' is where Sylvia must go; and she must show him her beauty is her appetite for life. In the back of the car are her sensible street clothes and shoes. But at least she's made sure her face is powdered and her lips are full and red. And her hair is curled.

*   *   *

It's like interference on a radio, the crackle of Sylvia's impending arrival. Although she's not expected, he can feel it in the electric touch of the doorknob, the crazy signals that come in the window from the neon lights of strip parlours, the sudden shadow cast by Assia

149

before she walks in. Now she stands, arms akimbo, in her gown of flame-coloured silk, and asks him what he's doing pacing up and down the room like this. She could be speaking in Sanskrit or whistling like the bright macaw he's begun to see her as now. But still he's caught, in the land he's invented for her— the land of voluptuousness and temptation, the lust bazaar.

'You will tell Sylvia, won't you?' As always, Assia's refined Knightsbridge accent jars with her exotic appearance—and, for that matter, with her intelligence and personality, these acknowledged by her lover only on occasion. 'You promised you'd tell her. Please—for God's sake, do!'

Ted already knows, as his eye adds to the plumpness of Assia, watches her harem walk, proud stretching of limbs and extending of stomach, that this baby will kill Sylvia. Assia's baby, dark and pleading, lies for a moment, to his imagination, in her arms, neon lights playing on matted hair, closed eyes. He shudders. But he's promised—and now it's late and he must go. He's forgotten he felt Sylvia on her way here, he dismisses the idea when it visits—this isn't a landscape for Sylvia, not at all.

'Yes, I'll tell her.' He doesn't say he already has, in so many words. And he sees the hare he ran over and killed, as its blood turns to flowers and the bouquet blossoms in his lover's hand. Portents, dreams—they're thick in the air here, in the flat that can be his for only a short while before he and the woman he has fallen so disastrously in love with have to move on. He sees them, poor, going from door to door—and he goes to kiss Assia before walking out onto the dark stairs.

Both of them know, as he draws in breath at the shock of volts that attacks his hand on the handle of the door, that the electric current comes from Sylvia. And in that moment, as the tingling in his fingers goes right up into his heart, Ted knows he loves her.

* * *

Sylvla parks the car with difficulty, in this strange new country where the lights are so bright and snow has melted or perhaps never settled there. But then, after all, this is hell. The feet of hookers tap along the pavements, loud in the sudden silence after she's turned off the engine. Good, trusty car! Where does she leave you? Were you ever found again, after the movements and promises and words of the next three days were decoded or misunderstood? Or do cars disappear, as the dead are said to do in this place of sin, buried in concrete or crushed to a pulp and thrown away? Sylvia is in no mood to care. She knows, as Ted does, that her story can have two endings. One is love and the other is death.

Soho is everything that is red, everything Sylvia has dreamed of when she pines for love in the white wastes of Fitzroy Road. Sex is everywhere, here: in red it's blazoned ten feet high on wires across sooty buildings; in red it walks on high stiletto heels, tap, tap. From restaurants where red-and-white-checked tablecloths are laid out for the evening meal comes the promise and smell of sex: garlic, French bread, red wine. And Sylvia transforms into her double, the dark woman with the lure of sex, as she finds the door beside the shop and pushes it open and goes up.

There's Ted, just as she knew he would be, coming down the dusty stairs toward her. They both halt in their tracks.

Ted has to smile: that nervous, thin smile that's like a child's scribble on a magic erasing slate: now here, now gone.

'Come on up!' he says.

*　　　*　　　*

As soon as Sylvia climbs the stairs, he knows them all to be in great danger. She's composed, her hair is curled, and peeping from the unbuttoned top of her overcoat is the metallic blue-black that signals, for Ted, the onset of trouble. Sylvia is going somewhere—indeed, she announces, without bothering to turn around on the dusty steps, which stink of

152

garlic and sour wine from the restaurant beneath, that she hasn't long. 'I'm expected somewhere,' she says. The door is slightly open and she places her hand on it as if—so the thought comes to him—she is pushing at the entrance to a tomb.

Assia, uneducated, bursting and burgeoning in the neon colours she wears in Sylvia's dreams, pulls open the door with a jerk. She and Sylvia stand staring at each other and they know themselves to be the other, two sides of a German past that will never be over—which melds and unites them in refusal of memory, in pain and desire. Ted is on the stairs still, maddened, regretting the visit he had paid to Sylvia in Fitzroy Road and the unspoken fact of Assia's baby. But it's impossible to confront, so he puts it out of his mind. To be caught perilously on a staircase is too reminiscent of the time in Devon when the telephone rang— and, as in a domestic comedy, he fell headlong down the stairs, almost was killed, in his haste to receive the adulterous call. Sylvia's mother had been watching, so he remembers, from the wings—the door into the kitchen at Court Green.

'Have a drink,' Ted says to Sylvia. He's in the room now, and notes that she refuses to look around at the fixtures and fittings, usually of great interest to her, if only in order to despise them later. He hopes she won't refer to the flat's squalor: already Assia exhibits the symptoms of class terror, rearing back and emitting a long, hostile hiss, as if the thought of competition with Sylvia is out of order here. Despite, as Ted wearily thinks, the fact that Assia more than anyone is aware of her standing in society—if she has one at all—and is fervently keen to marry him and become the wife of a poet already the recipient of recognition and honours.

'I wanted to see you,' Sylvia says directly across the room. She speaks into a darkness that seems to grow with the February evening, the absence of the snow-fight she's become accustomed to, up in freezing Hampstead. 'I came to see if you were here.'

There really is no end to this impasse. Neither Sylvia's husband nor his mistress has the courage to come right out with the news. Like many women blamed for their husbands' desertion, Sylvia hesitates fatally and stares down into the chasm of her uncertainty, self-loathing, and combined love and hatred for the man she married, thus finding herself powerless once again. Her composure melts in the heat of her humiliation. For surely, as all three stand there silent—and Sylvia shakes her head once more when proffered a glass of wine—the evidence must be before her of Assia's condition, her shame and guilt and joy. There is nothing for Sylvia to do but leave. Nothing to say but to repeat, like an idiot, that she has to leave now—and, she adds, in a cab, are there any in this street? She'd really rather not take the car.

There is little more aggravating to one caught up in the scene that changes lives, the most compelling scene in the drama, than the sudden intervention of a practical note—particularly if that practicality is transparently based on opportunism. 'In that case,' Ted says, 'I'll take the car, bring it back Monday, okay?'

'Won't you stay?' says Assia, and it does sound as if she really means it. Perhaps she does. The two women are joined, and it's hard for either of them to part. Besides, they've been balked of the scene. Neither likes the way Ted has jumped at the car.

Sylvia doesn't hesitate this time. Maybe it's her only chance, and she knows it, of snubbing the exotic stranger whose books on the Cabala are lying on the table by the window, with Hebrew books of poetry strewn on the floor by the bed. (But Sylvia won't look at the bed.)

'It's out of the question,' is her reply. She leaves the room quietly and at speed. Assia's hurt and anger follow her down to the battered front door and out into the street.

*   *   *

Syivia holds her knowledge, her icy knowledge of the fact of Assia's baby, within like an icicle, a poison-tipped needle, as she seeks and finds a taxi, gives the address in a clipped, matter-of-fact tone. She will never allow the pointed, agonising tip to move inside her. She will carry it like the victim of a murder who knows there is no way to find relief from the pain. She is in a jungle, a jungle where the creepers are of ice. But—and she has a dreadful happiness, a hilarity as well at the obvious outcome of her silent confrontation in Soho—she has a retaliation waiting, after all. She's so glad, she tells herself, that she planned this in advance.

The cab goes slowly across London. But when it arrives at the friend's house—the friend she had counted on, who might have shown his love and sympathy for her—the house is in darkness and there is nobody there.

*   *   *

It's late when she gets back to the Beckers' in Islington. But what does it matter now, when she has this new, fatal gift to wear inside, a vest with a thousand hairs, each one sticking in her ribs and impossible to extract. The important thing is to keep her new knowledge to herself alone. With the Beckers she is calm and competent, and they will remember this in three days' time when questioned repeatedly on the state of Mrs Hughes.

She seemed to have made up her mind about something. As if a matter that had been bothering her was at last settled. That is the gist of the Beckers' message to the inquirers.

156

Sylvia's composure, as they were keen to stress, was unlike the wretched state she'd been in before driving over to Fitzroy Road. No, they had no idea where she could have left the car.

The Old Man and the Woman Upstairs

Professor Trevor Thomas is tired of the young woman and her mad behaviour, not to mention her complaints. Shopping, the weather, the lateness of a girl coming to help look after the children: everything in life is impossible for this wife and mother who was so keen to point out to him the other night that she is in fact the author of a novel and not just Mrs Hughes. Why should he care if her husband went off with a wicked woman? It all sounds invented, somehow, and ever since he found her sitting in her car in the freezing cold one dark early evening, sitting there for at least an hour, he's known she's off her head. He should have her flat for himself and his sons. If this craziness goes on—and Dr Harder, who treats the professor and most people in this area, has given her an anti-depressant medication, he knows that from the rubbish bins no one comes to empty in this atrocious weather—if this mad act continues, she'll be out and the flat will be his, he's sure of it. 'Just thinking,' the crazy woman had replied when he'd taken the trouble and crossed the ice rink that is Fitzroy Road to ask her if she was all right in there. Just thinking! For an hour in an unheated car! Professor Thomas wonders if maybe he should call Dr Harder and tell him about the episode. But what she needs most is her husband back, and the professor has had a good mind to summon him over instead of Dr Harder, and suggest they both move out of the flat. It was false pretences, anyway: the two of them were meant to live there, and now there's just the self-obsessed woman and her kids.

Tonight Professor Thomas doesn't open his door—and he thinks it's really going too far when Mrs Hughes comes down and asks if she can buy stamps off him. Stamps! At this hour! Insisting on paying for them then and there and talking about God and her conscience just prolongs things horribly in the draughty hall.

Really, that's all Professor Thomas remembers. He suffered further inconvenience, of course, when in the early hours of the morning the gas came down through the floorboards just as the voices had, and he was obliged to take off two days at the gallery where he's part-time as a result of inhaling the fumes as he slept. But few sympathised with the old man, though many were avid to know what happened, after the death.

The boy dances along the ledge high above the valley, his foot dislodging small stones, flint-shaped, that fly like arrows down the side of the ravine. As he runs, he grows, and his breath comes faster, choking in the sudden understanding of his responsibility and grief. By the time dusk has come late to the northern moor he is fully grown and his steps drag—descending, descending to the churchyard and the shell-decked grave. He is neither man nor boy now: wings, grey and heavy as a gander's, bear him up again, on a lost air current, and carry him back to the big city in the south, to the woman he can no longer love.

Then he wakes. There was a party, clearly: glasses half-empty, blood-rimmed with wine. Scarves in soft chiffon and silk, a Persian robe that makes a fragile cocoon for Assia. Light comes in, as it did yesterday and the day before, as for Sylvia it never will again. Ted sleeps once more, a boy dancing along a ledge high above the valley.

The Nurse's Tale

Two women came, it was said, to the house when the snow was melting and the first London crocuses—as grimy as the birds that pecked at them and then flew on—pushed up on winter-starved grass in the garden of Fitzroy Road.

The first woman was a nurse—she had a knowing face, the second woman, Elizabeth, Sylvia's old friend from Devon, said. She had a black bag with her. Not a children's nurse, the children were out for the day and maybe longer. When she stood on the step and pressed the bell, she saw that the curtains of the ground-floor room were still drawn. Clouds, as white as the gauze and soft cotton-wool the nurse had in her bag, gathered overhead.

The door was answered by a young girl, an au pair the nurse thought she must be, and as soon as the nurse had come into the hall and started to go up the stairs, the young girl ran out into the street. The nurse paused a while, as if a trace of the old man on the ground floor—a scent of his sharp, elbow-swinging walk, his keen, spying glance—had lingered there and played itself out without knowing how to stop, in this house of tragedy.

Then she went on. Up the stairs the dead woman had been carried down—three weeks past, but the nurse knew nothing of that. She came for another. Now she takes the dark climb to the bedroom where a strip of half-stitched scarlet corduroy still lies on the chair at the bed's head. As she walks in she hears wolves howl in the zoo, down the road in the leafless park. The woman now in the bed is not the mistress of this cold, forbidding flat—nor is she the seamstress of the corduroy that was intended for the windows of the sitting room. She is a stranger here—though the nurse, on her first and only visit to Fitzroy Road, has no way of knowing this. She is unaware that the woman who lies in bed in the room where the light bulb, too hastily thrust into its socket, trembles in the overhead lampshade has found her worst nightmare come true. For she, Little Red Riding Hood, her father's favourite, heroine of the fairy tale they both loved and feared—is lying here emptied out, bleeding, while the wolves across the park bay in the late, violet March dusk. The story has twisted and contorted again, so there can be no happy ending.

The nurse is quick and efficient with Mrs Wevill—as she has been informed is her patient's name. Stirrup marks are still visible on the buttocks and thighs of a woman the nurse sees is beautiful, logging this as she squeezes the pelvis, then going back and forth to the glacial bathroom. This is a beauty that goes with weeping: skin freckle-spattered, as if washed by a Saharan downpour; black hair like a curtain of crushed flies and spiders, enmeshed in a fatal war game. The eyes: they're wet still with tears, but the great pale irises fringed with black that look helplessly up at her make the nurse shake her head—though whether in sympathy or disdain it would be hard to say. 'Just turn this way, Mrs Wevill—that's it, that's a good girl.' So many abortions badly done like this: idly, the nurse wonders if it's Dr Maher's clinic in Hendon that's to blame for this mess again. Then the bedroom door opens and a man comes in, his entrance disturbed almost at once by a doorbell ringing downstairs, piercing and long. The nurse hardly has a chance to glimpse the man, the tall handsome woodcutter who has come to cut Red Riding Hood free. She has a feeling, though she doesn't know where it comes from, that the man may be the wolf—who bites his victim's entrails while pretending to be her grandmother. The woman in the bed sees him—for she cries out—and then mutters about her father and mother—and the nurse wonders if she's delirious, despite a temperature that's not too high. The man doesn't answer, but turns on his heel and goes out. Someone must have opened the front door into Fitzroy Road because steps can now be heard, coming up the stairs as far as the kitchen. And in response to a remark from the man—the wolves again, the nurse hears him say: how they howl all night and keep him from his sleep—a murmur of understanding, a silence the nurse can tell is filled with sighs. Then the man's voice: harsh this time, angry in his sorrow: 'It seems appropriate, after all.'

When the nurse reaches the kitchen she

sees the new visitor, a pretty woman, slightly out of breath, with a kind face. The au pair is there as well, and the nurse sees that it was the young girl who, on returning, admitted the kind woman to this house where the curtains of a tired grey brocade, in the downstairs room, were drawn even at midday. The nurse bustles to the sink to fill a kettle for her patient. There are too many women in the kitchen, and she stumbles slightly, up against the tall handsome man. He is talking to the new visitor: she is Elizabeth Compton and she is full of concern and grief. 'I'm sorry,' she says, 'I'm so sorry.' And then she looks around for the children and her shoulders droop. 'It's a door closing,' says the man Elizabeth calls Ted, repeating the name on a sigh, 'a steel door closing.' Then he hands her a book; the nurse sees it has The Bell Jar written on the outside and that the woman called Elizabeth weeps when he says, 'Sylvia dedicated this to you.' And he backs away, and goes up the stairs—to the wounded woman, the woman who cries half-asleep of a street in Berlin and a father who can do nothing to save her now.

The kind woman stares at the kettle as it goes on the burner. The nurse searches for a match, to light the gas: she hears the visitor's sharp intake of breath as the ring of flames, yellow and blue, hisses and roars in a sudden silence. What was the trouble? the nurse wonders. Some households you're hard put to

163

it to find a match. And these were on the shelf above the cooker, just where you'd expect to find them. There's only two or three left—and the tall man doesn't look good at remembering details of household supplies. But the nurse doesn't know that Mrs Hughes knelt here, just where the nurse is standing, and folded a cloth before placing it on a shelf in the oven, and then put her head on the cloth and turned on the gas. She hadn't used a match. 'Where are the children?' the kind woman says, as if she knows that the hissing, quieted now with the kettle sitting on the ring but too audible all the same, must be overlaid by the present, by question and answer.

The au pair replies that they're out, but she doesn't say with whom or when they'll be back. 'She's here,' the girl goes on; and the nurse, only half-listening, goes to the window and looking out sees another sheet of rain, whitened by hail and sleet, as it drives across the road and over the house, where the mirrors went white as if smothered by a blanket at the time of the death of the poet. 'Who?' asks the kind woman, looking apprehensively at the little staircase leading up to the bedroom. 'Oh, Mrs Wevill,' says the girl. 'She's up there, in bed.' Now the pretty woman with the kind face seems to understand, and she glances at the nurse and then again at the kettle, which lets out a shriek as it comes to the boil. The sound darts around the kitchen with its tightly closed windows. The nurse lifts the hot-water bottle, ready by the side of the cooker, and goes to turn off the gas. 'What's wrong with her?' the visitor wants to be told; and when the girl rolls her eyes and says, 'Oh, you know', the nurse feels impelled to speak at last. 'You can't keep a good woman down,' the nurse says as she rolls back the red rubber lips of the hot-water bottle and directs the scalding water deep into its belly. And as she goes in the new silence the extinguished gas has made there—as she stands by the window to let the handsome man come down the narrow stairs— she sees that he is weeping—she leans right up against the window pane to look out. In the rain that is like a child's scribbling against the slate grey sky, the muffled-up figure of old Professor Thomas makes its way out of the house and across the road. The nurse wonders if he knows the story that lies behind this strange household; but by the time she has laid the warm bottle in its pink knitted cover across the stomach of her charge in the room upstairs, she has forgotten all about him. She looks straight ahead when she takes her leave ten minutes later, for the handsome man in the kitchen still weeps, and accuses himself, to the kind woman, of all manner of things. 'It doesn't fall to many, to murder a genius,' he says. And the nurse leaves, saying she'll be back tomorrow—or maybe it'll be someone else on duty then, depending on the district nurses' roster.

The Secretary's Tale

You can't keep a good woman down. It was like something in the ads, written by the agency Assia now works for, J. Walter Thompson. Jennifer was only 'a humble secretary' there, as she will relate to the curious, the prurient, seven years later—and she had never met anyone so clever, so downright glamorous, so exceedingly beautiful as Assia Wevill.

There might have been a husband, or a boyfriend—or maybe both—but they were never spoken about. For Jennifer, a magic carpet unrolled when you listened to Assia, and a host of treasures spilled out—something like that, something that made you think of a high-profile ad. For the life, the glittering façade, of this lovely creature was that of a woman you just couldn't keep down. (Unless, though Jennifer wasn't good at noticing them, you saw the depressions come in like weather fronts in semicircles under the pale eyes, and you saw the bruises grow, widening like water where petrol has been thrown in.)

Jennifer might have seen the psychic wounds, but she did not. There was the office, the coffee machine, the hum of laughter and excitement around Assia's desk, when new, impossible ideas were spewed out. She was clever, Assia, and endlessly inventive. It was a saucy time, with Cliveden swimming pools and blondes with cotton-candy hair, and a Cabinet Minister's mistress photographed naked on a harp-backed chair. Assia could sniff the new era dawning. Assia was the new era, vulnerable, self-regarding, generous with pity and love. Something like that, like magazine copy for women of a new age.

Today Jennifer and Assia are enjoying their weekly lunch at an expensive restaurant. Assia 'whisks off' the secretary who admires her silently all week long, waiting for the sudden pounce, the trip to San Frediano, or Meridiana, or Alvaro's in the King's Road. Chelsea! That's Assia, that's where she loves to go. Assia, with her kohl-rimmed eyes, eyes like shallow lakes in a face freckled the colour of sand, is an exotic import in the restaurants and boutiques of the King's Road.

If it's not easy to see the suffering, the odd, thrilling blend of impatience and sadness, in Assia, it's because she doesn't speak of the future—or of the present, for that matter, except in the most brittle and superficial ways. She retells the past—and on this sunny Thursday, as she and Jennifer sit behind their wattle fence of bread-sticks and pepper grinders, hidden from and revealed to a world gasping as ever at Assia's beauty—she speaks again of the childhood and family from which

167

her beauty and mystery must come. On this occasion, Lonya, her father, is a Russian prince; and Jennifer stares and listens and stares, as the pasta, little envelopes wrapped discreetly around spinach and ricotta, sits untasted on her idol's plate. 'Escaping from Russia—he's there with the great ruby buried in, of all things, a pot of cold cream, and he's in a train. But when it stops at the border . . .' Escaping from Berlin—and here the face that is all sympathy and imagination, planes of understanding, a perfection of feature that needs neither correction nor cut, grows sombre, for she, Assia, was a part of this fleeing. 'We went at night. My aunt was too late, at the station . . .' And the wonderful face droops in a darkness that has grown around the table in the chic brightness—'But let me explain to you what my Father did in the forests, when he was in Russia before the Revolution, hunting bears . . .' Jennifer, overcome, stares and listens on.

There has to be a novel plan, at each of these lunches (from which Jennifer emerges intoxicated not by wine but by 'the colourful past', as she describes it, of Assia's making). There will surely come an idea, to amuse and entertain for a short while; and today's, inspired by the granita, the coffee ice Assia now tackles with a long spoon, has all the impracticality and wild affection of which Assia is capable. 'All we need, Jenny dear, is an

168

old refrigerator'—here the cut-glass accent peels back a little, to show Germanic r's beneath—'a fridge, and a van big enough to take it. You know someone with these things, Jenny, don't you?'

'But what for?' Jenny asks, as a waiter, brushing by her (for she is invisible next to Assia), causes her glass to shake perilously on the tabletop. Assia is laughing her delicious laugh. She is as coffee-coloured now as the gritty concoction she consumes. 'Oh, Jenny, to hand out ice-cream, of course. To the children on Hampstead Heath. Children will love it, in this hot weather, don't you think? Free, of course, completely free.'

Jenny doesn't know anyone with a refrigerator or a van. But she sees in her mind's eye the beautiful lady on the Heath, like an oracle in a clearing, obscured by the shimmer of heat in the long, green day. And she sees the van, rickety and lopsided. (But where can she find one? Immediately she feels herself inadequate, with this princess from a lost country, an Anastasia given over to advertising: how can she ensure that these lunches go on and on?) 'Never mind,' Assia says, and her friend sees that her eyes have filled with tears. 'I love children so much. I'm quite old, Jenny. How old do you think I am?'

The secretary remembers all this—but then the lunches become rarer and the lacunae in the memory produce white vans and invented

169

ice-cream festivals and the time (it must have been so much later) when Assia sat across a table in a restaurant in Fulham Road and tried to make a joke of her terrible isolation. 'I rattle with loneliness, Jenny.' Could she have said that? It's true, though the secretary doesn't like to admit it, that Assia has aged and put on weight. She's been away, living in the country: she no longer 'whisks off' her friend but has to come in from Clapham on the tube, and she has to make baby-sitting arrangements before she can do even that. But the two women stick to their original, unspoken arrangement: there will be little mention of the present; and of the future, none at all.

It is different this day, though. The myriad scenarios for unwritten books, the genealogical revelations and fantasies, all seem to have died away. 'I put in an ad in a lonely-hearts column, Jenny,' says the woman the other lunchers still stare at—but almost angrily, as if they can see her beauty and slenderness disappear before their eyes. 'What do you think of that?' And, as this is met with silence, not the habitual silence of adoration but one of incredulity, almost of fear, Assia goes on: 'Don't you think I deserve a man?' And her voice picks up as her imagination begins once more to explore the possibilities of a novel's plot. 'An older man, white-haired, in a library in a country house—who wants to look after a woman and

170

a child. A widower, perhaps . . .' But here her voice drops, and she sits at the table in the restaurant in Fulham Road as silently as her friend.

*   *   *

Loaves and fishes. That's what Jenny thinks as she queues at the supermarket, shifts a bag already heavy with the wild strawberries Assia has sent her to find in Harrods, tries to decipher the writing with its foreign-looped f's and s's, each word as emphatic and desperate as the writer has lately become. Surely, the faithful secretary muses, one of the incomparable Assia Wevill's plots—for a novel, a film script, a long poem to beat her rival's morbid outpourings—surely one of these ventures will sooner or later be realised and fame and fortune will result. Assia looks like a celebrity: secretly, it's a disappointment to Jenny and others at the office that she isn't already one. So many young directors out there, in their low-slung sports cars, who would take the Russian-German beauty out of the forest and make her a star . . . such a plethora of publishers (Jenny sees them sometimes when they come in to J. Walter Thompson, exuding superiority over the brash world of advertising) who would rush her heroine into print. Assia could take her pick of any of them. The fact that she seems stuck on this poet who doesn't even earn very much is beginning to get Jenny's goat. There's no mention of him, that's suspicious in itself. But every time the kind-faced accommodating girl who edges her way past new, thin bundles of asparagus and farm-brown eggs to the till tries to build a plot for herself, one that will contain the dumping of the current boyfriend and the acquisition of another, better man who will carry Assia to recognition, reality sets in. She pays—it's a massive bill and she knows Assia won't get any of it back from Mr Hughes. He's the love of her life, though. Jenny, arms aching from the weight of the shopping, staggers across the pavement to the bus stop.

Loaves and fishes turns out to be right: despite the massive amount of food and wine, more guests come than had been bargained for. 'Oh, Jenny, I'm so sorry—just the little shop down the road—some Uncle Ben's will do—while you're there, a bottle of tequila— why is it so hard to get sea salt in bloody Clapham?'

Jenny doesn't mind the extra work because this will give her a chance to see the set-up Assia keeps quiet about. So much talk about Russian princes and German fairy tales— about the children who had been friends in Tel Aviv and the huge places they lived in now in the south of France, where Assia can go whenever she tires of this cold, dim place she has ended up in. But never a word about Ted.

172

And there's a child—she never talks about that, either—though Jenny has been told by Alice, a friendly office gossip, that it's a girl. Now, tonight, after the shock of seeing for the first time the bareness and sadness of the flat where this exotic, otherworldly creature is forced to live, comes the chance to check out how this superior being is treated in her own home.

The off-licence (very like the impractical Assia Wevill not to have noticed) is closed and Jenny has to take a bus down to the Broadway. Tequila doesn't exist in Clapham—like the ads constructed and then jettisoned by her idol on a bad day, it's a fantasy no one else can participate in. Absentmindedly, Jenny finds and buys sea salt anyway, and she sees Assia's impatient reception of the white grains, packaged in a long canister with pictures of a faraway blue ocean. 'Why bring nothing but the salt, for heaven's sake?' But a flashing smile comes after the reprimand, in Jenny's imagination; and sure enough, when she has bought French bread (a good mark for this) and two large packets of Uncle Ben's, it goes exactly as she had foreseen. The only difference is, as Assia makes her petulant remark about the absence of tequila and the folly of bringing only salt, a man comes out of the bedroom in the flat and stands staring at Jenny in the cramped hall.

The secretary always pauses at this point in

173

her tale. She doesn't like to give a description of the man who was the love of her friend's life, the man who went on to cause her death. The secretary goes off, here, into the wine vinegar she was then asked to provide, as if with a magic wand, when a huge salad (this mixed by the man) was found to be without the *vinaigre de vin* (Assia is shouting the words in French as if to outsmart him by showing her greater level of sophistication) needed to go on the leaves. And the doorbell is ringing. The kitchen is tiny. It has grown very hot. Jenny fears for the wild strawberries, which have turned purple and blue, small contusions she now places too late in the overfilled fridge. Then a child runs in.

The great shame, as Elizabeth the house sitter and dweller in the Devon village will proclaim—the worst shame of the whole business was the life of the child. She was made unhappy by her mother's inability to cope with her own unhappiness. The child had dark hair and eyes and her head drooped when she sat on her mother's knee. Even the secretary, in the midst of the preparations she had somehow known she would have to make—'Oh, Jenny darling, please can you put on the rice? Sweetie, I can't get my hands all covered in oil—I think we need to make a ratatouille, can you find the aubergine and the zucchini?'—even in the chaos of Assia's flat, she could tell that the child lacked reassurance

174

from her mother. There would be no finger, sugar-coated, held out for her to lick. The man, the poet whom her goddess Assia will never leave, is looking down at Shura—Jenny hears the name and she finds it haunting: long after mother and child are both dead she will whisper the name to herself—Shura, Shura—and he is looking at her as if the double burden of a neurotic woman and her daughter is more than he can bear. Jenny, nervous, takes a handful of strawberries from the fridge and hands them out.

'You know,' she says in the office, months after that sad evening, 'my memory of dinner at Assia's is of too many people crowded in too little space. She went in and out of the kitchen with the bowls of rice, and the man carried out the salad in a big green bowl. Assia Wevill never took her eyes off him. Some of them sat at a round table, and the rest sat on sofas and chairs. The child wandered about and her mother and father didn't seem to notice her at all.'

Alice from the office came, rather late, and she joined Jenny in the kitchen after the food had been served. 'I think it's a shame,' Alice said, and the word 'shame' began to echo in the secretary's ears, as it would for years to come. 'I could have gone in there and brought the child out,' Alice said. 'She could have come in the kitchen and been happier, you know. But somehow—he has such a magnetic force—did you see it, Jenny?—somehow I just went in and sat down at dinner and ignored her along with the rest.'

The House Sitter's Tale

They came to take some things from the house. It was all a question of giving and taking. Because already you could see that the dead were stronger than the living—and for each thing they took, something far more important was snatched back.

She didn't see it at first, says Elizabeth, who was the first wife's friend. Elizabeth, who was there the day the nurse came to the house where he hears the wolves howl all night. She thought she had everything, and then could take more. But he—he knew the same story was playing out, and there was nothing he could do to pull down the curtain. They came to Devon that day when all the daffodils—for which the place was famous—were blooming. And he took the strawberry plants, in a coalscuttle. A rug, too. Quite a big rug.

There were three acts, as Elizabeth describes them; and they were all to do with the presence of the woman they thought had gone from their lives. It's like that, isn't it? At the Devon house, he weeps as he kneels on the floor, tying up the rug. And she—she asks if

176

she can have a guided tour of the premises, as if she's thinking of buying or coming to settle here. She was self-confident then, even if he was crying, kneeling on the bare boards with a rug and a coalscuttle filled with strawberry plants. Show me the house, Elizabeth, she says—but I see she's put out by the tears her man sheds—after all, he's in love with her, isn't he?

So Elizabeth takes her up the stairs. The rival, who has been foolish enough already to criticise the simple meal of mince and potatoes the house sitter and her husband have provided, calling it a 'nursery meal' in that ridiculous Knightsbridge accent of hers. The rival who has stepped into the shoes of Elizabeth's friend Sylvia.

The house is still crimson and white. Since the split, nothing has mended and death has solved nothing here or anywhere else.

The stairs repel, it's like trying to climb a cliff face. But Elizabeth struggles on. She knows that Assia Wevill must have a good idea of the layout of the place: after all, she came to visit here just a year ago or less and he went off to London after her. 'Elizabeth'—her friend hears the voice, sees the gaunt face a hundred times a day. 'When the freeze is over I'm coming down,' she'd said. 'In time for the daffodils.' But now this one has come instead. She's not content with taking the husband, she's taking plants out of the ground, too.

Yet there's something in this house that is stronger than the woman who looks so foreign in this landscape. It stops them both in their tracks—as if in obedience to Elizabeth's unspoken thought, that all this showing around is really an expression of triumph, a need for him to see her taken into the room where the poems came gushing out. The showing is designed as a demonstration of a rival's power so that the house sitter is bound to take the key from her pocket and place it in the lock of the door. But another voice has come to possess the new owner of the man who cries in the kitchen.' Don't you feel rather a traitor?' Assia says as they stand, inexplicably unable to move on the hard scarlet carpet of the steps: 'Taking me to her room, I mean.' And, as in a dance choreographed long before, Elizabeth turns and leads the way down the stairs. Assia follows her.

So, as the house sitter remembers, the power shifts again, the house stands firm and square and denies invaders the right to enter, to snoop and pry. Assia turns to Elizabeth as they return to the kitchen, the smell of mince, the herbs Sylvia tied and hung on the wall the summer before dried and blackened by the long cold months. She turns to the woman she has already snubbed; and her voice is different, low, cracked with uncertainty and fear. 'Can Ted and I be happy together?' she says, like an actress who realises, suddenly, that she has no belief in her lines.

'Look at him!' is all Elizabeth can reply.

* * *

Sea witch, Elizabeth says. That was the name of the hair dye Assia bought. A kind of bluish-black; he told everyone she was going grey, she was older than him, you know.

She was so unhappy when she came to take possession of the house at last. Her child was sad, too.

And as time went by, everything was taken from her. She went back to London—it was no good for her in an English village, she was like a stranger, and when Christmas came and she baked a Russian Christmas cake, he rang, desperate for us to come and eat it with her: she was so lonely and depressed.

Everything she had taken was taken back from her, and more. Love, youth, finally her child's life and her own, seven years after that first visit to the poets in Devon.

He watched the play he knew so well: the grief mask, the child, the implorings—then the chill, the stupor, and the letting go.

* * *

It was seven years later, after the death of Assia and her murder of her child, that people started to see the birds up on the Heath. You can still see them if you go at dusk, in the month of May. They fly over trees high above the city and then disappear, into the night. A swallow, a nightingale, and a hoopoe.

Acknowledgements

Elizabeth Sigmund, Sylvia Plath's best friend in the last year of her life, for her often tragic memories of the relationship.

Clarissa Roche, long-standing friend in the US and Britain of Sylvia Plath, who said of *Sylvia and Ted* that 'the insights are uncanny'.

Hilary Bailey, for her memories of Plath and her circle at Cambridge.

Alison Owen, producer of the film about Ted and Sylvia, who found 'psychological accuracy' in these pages.